THE FORCE AWAKENS: VOLUME 1

Luke Skywalker has vanished. In his absence, the sinister FIRST ORDER has risen from the ashes of the Empire and will not rest until Skywalker, the last Jedi, has been destroyed.

With the support of the REPUBLIC, General Leia Organa leads a brave RESISTANCE. She is desperate to find her brother Luke and gain his help in restoring peace and justice to the galaxy.

Leia has sent her most daring pilot on a secret mission to Jakku, where an old ally has discovered a clue to Luke's whereabouts....

CHUCK WENDIG
Writer

LUKE ROSS
Artist

FRANK MARTIN
Colorist

VC's CLAYTON COWLES
Letterer

ESAD RIBIC
Cover Artist

HEATHER ANTOS
Editor

JORDAN D. WHITE
Supervising Editor

C.B. CEBULSKI
Executive Editor

AXEL ALONSO
Editor In Chief

JOE QUESADA
Chief Creative Officer

DAN BUCKLEY
Publisher

Based on the screenplay by
LAWRENCE KASDAN & J.J. ABRAMS
and
MICHAEL ARNDT

For Lucasfilm:
Creative Director MICHAEL SIGLAIN
Senior Editor FRANK PARISI
Lucasfilm Story Group RAYNE ROBERTS, PABLO HIDALGO,
LELAND CHEE, MATT MARTIN

ABDO
Spotlight

ABDOPUBLISHING.COM

Reinforced library bound edition published in 2018 by Spotlight,
a division of ABDO, PO Box 398166, Minneapolis, Minnesota 55439.
Spotlight produces high-quality reinforced library bound editions for
schools and libraries. Published by agreement with Marvel Characters, Inc.

Printed in the United States of America, North Mankato, Minnesota.
042017
092017

THIS BOOK CONTAINS
RECYCLED MATERIALS

marvelkids.com

STAR WARS © & TM 2017 LUCASFILM LTD.

PUBLISHER'S CATALOGING IN PUBLICATION DATA

Names: Wendig, Chuck, author. | Ross, Luke ; Martin, Frank ; Laming, Marc,
  illustrators.
Title: The force awakens / writer: Chuck Wendig ; art: Luke Ross ; Frank Martin ;
  Marc Laming.
Description: Reinforced library bound edition. | Minneapolis, Minnesota : Spotlight,
  2018. | Series: Star wars : the force awakens | Volumes 1, 2, 4, 5, and 6 written
  by Chuck Wendig ; illustrated by Luke Ross & Frank Martin. | Volume 3 written
  by Chuck Wendig ; illustrated by Marc Laming & Frank Martin.
Summary: Three decades after the Rebel Alliance destroyed the Galactic Empire, a
  stirring in the Force brings young scavenger Rey, deserting Stormtrooper Finn,
  ace pilot Poe, and dark apprentice Kylo Ren's lives crashing together as the
  awakening begins.
Identifiers: LCCN 2016961930 | ISBN 9781532140228 (volume 1) | ISBN
  9781532140235 (volume 2) | ISBN 9781532140242 (volume 3) | ISBN
  9781532140259 (volume 4) | ISBN 9781532140266 (volume 5) | ISBN
  9781532140273 (volume 6)
Subjects: LCSH: Star Wars fiction--Comic book, strips, etc.--Juvenile fiction. |
  Space warfare--Juvenile fiction. | Adventure and adventurers--Juvenile fiction.
  Graphic novels--Juvenile fiction.
Classification: DDC 741.5--dc23
LC record available at https://lccn.loc.gov/2016961930

Spotlight

A Division of ABDO
abdopublishing.com

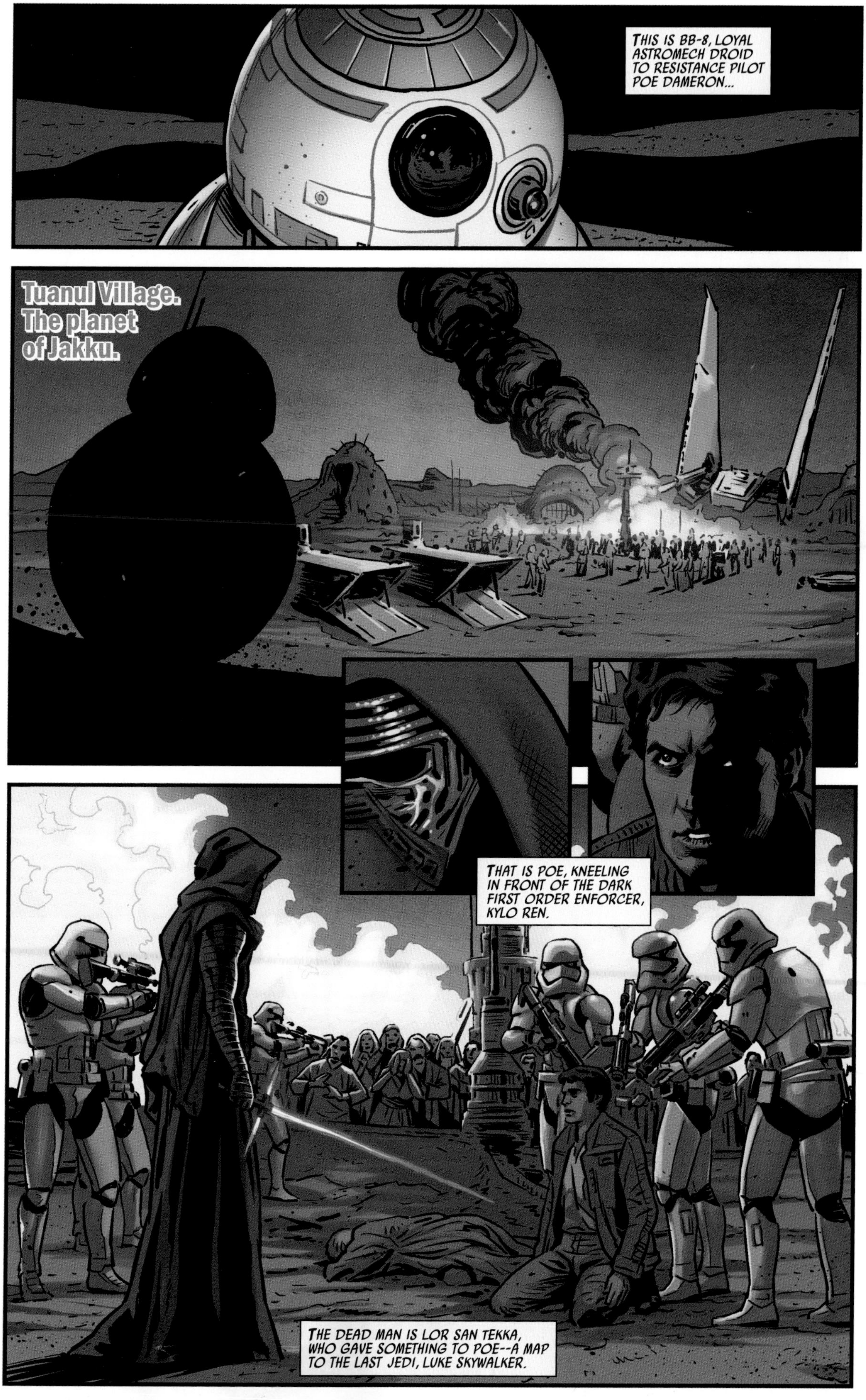
THIS IS BB-8, LOYAL ASTROMECH DROID TO RESISTANCE PILOT POE DAMERON...
Tuanul Village. The planet of Jakku.
THAT IS POE, KNEELING IN FRONT OF THE DARK FIRST ORDER ENFORCER, KYLO REN.
THE DEAD MAN IS LOR SAN TEKKA, WHO GAVE SOMETHING TO POE--A MAP TO THE LAST JEDI, LUKE SKYWALKER.

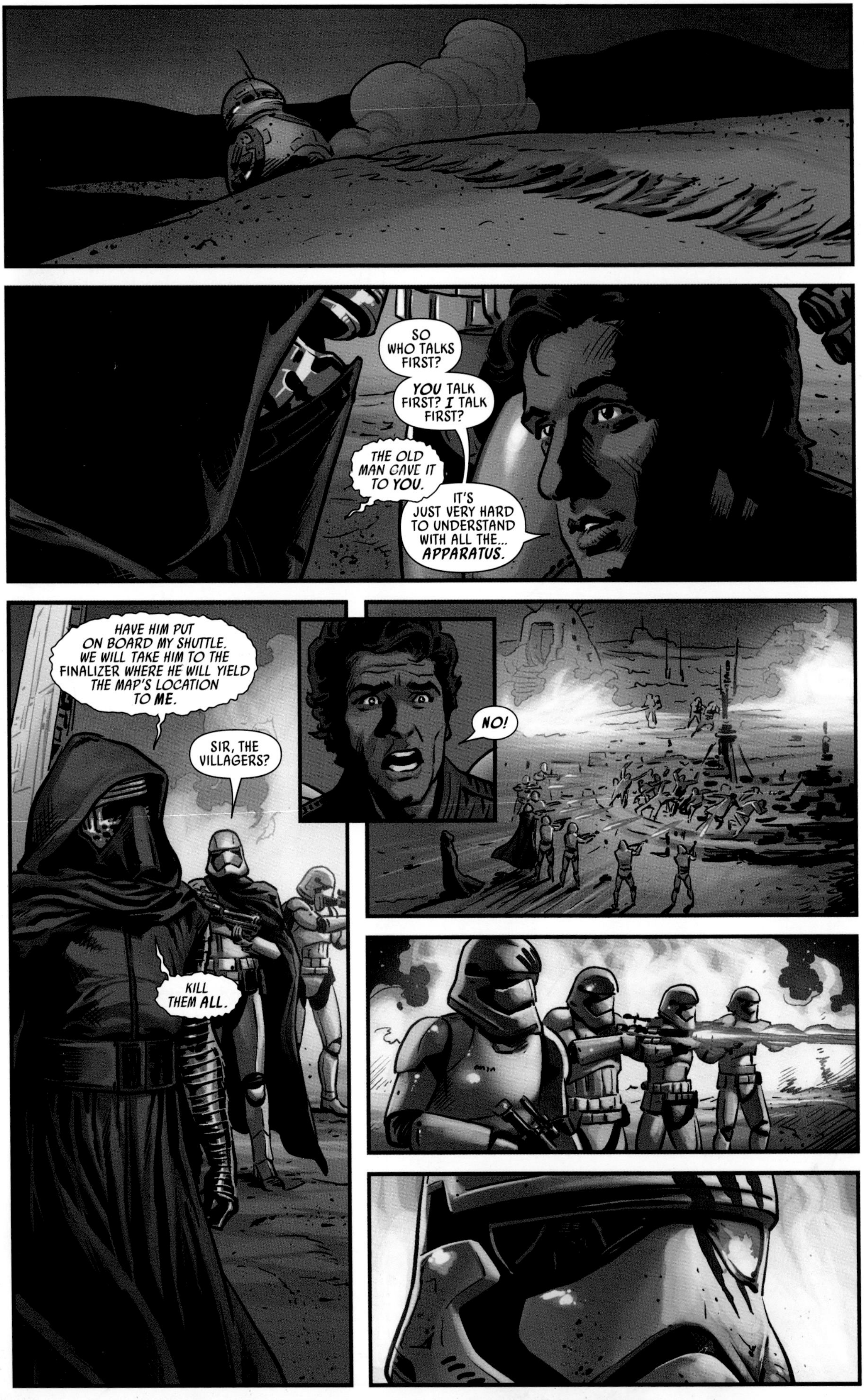
SO WHO TALKS FIRST?
YOU TALK FIRST? I TALK FIRST?
THE OLD MAN GAVE IT TO YOU.
IT'S JUST VERY HARD TO UNDERSTAND WITH ALL THE... APPARATUS.
HAVE HIM PUT ON BOARD MY SHUTTLE. WE WILL TAKE HIM TO THE FINALIZER WHERE HE WILL YIELD THE MAP'S LOCATION TO ME.
SIR, THE VILLAGERS?
KILL THEM ALL.
NO!

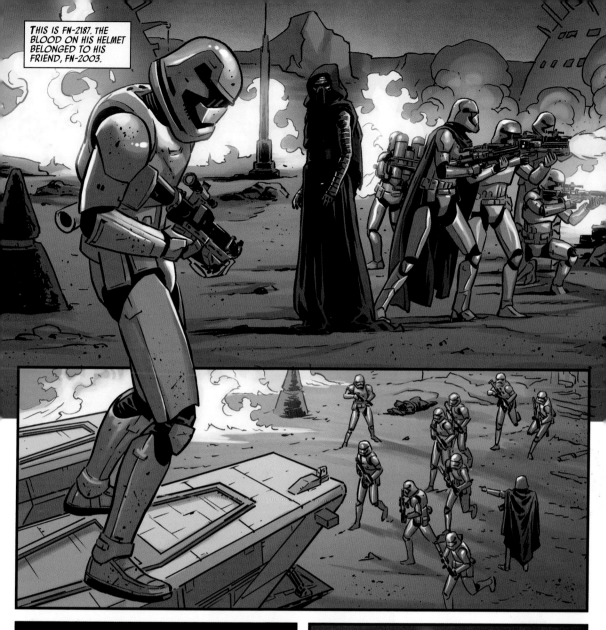

THIS IS FN-2187. THE BLOOD ON HIS HELMET BELONGED TO HIS FRIEND, FN-2003.

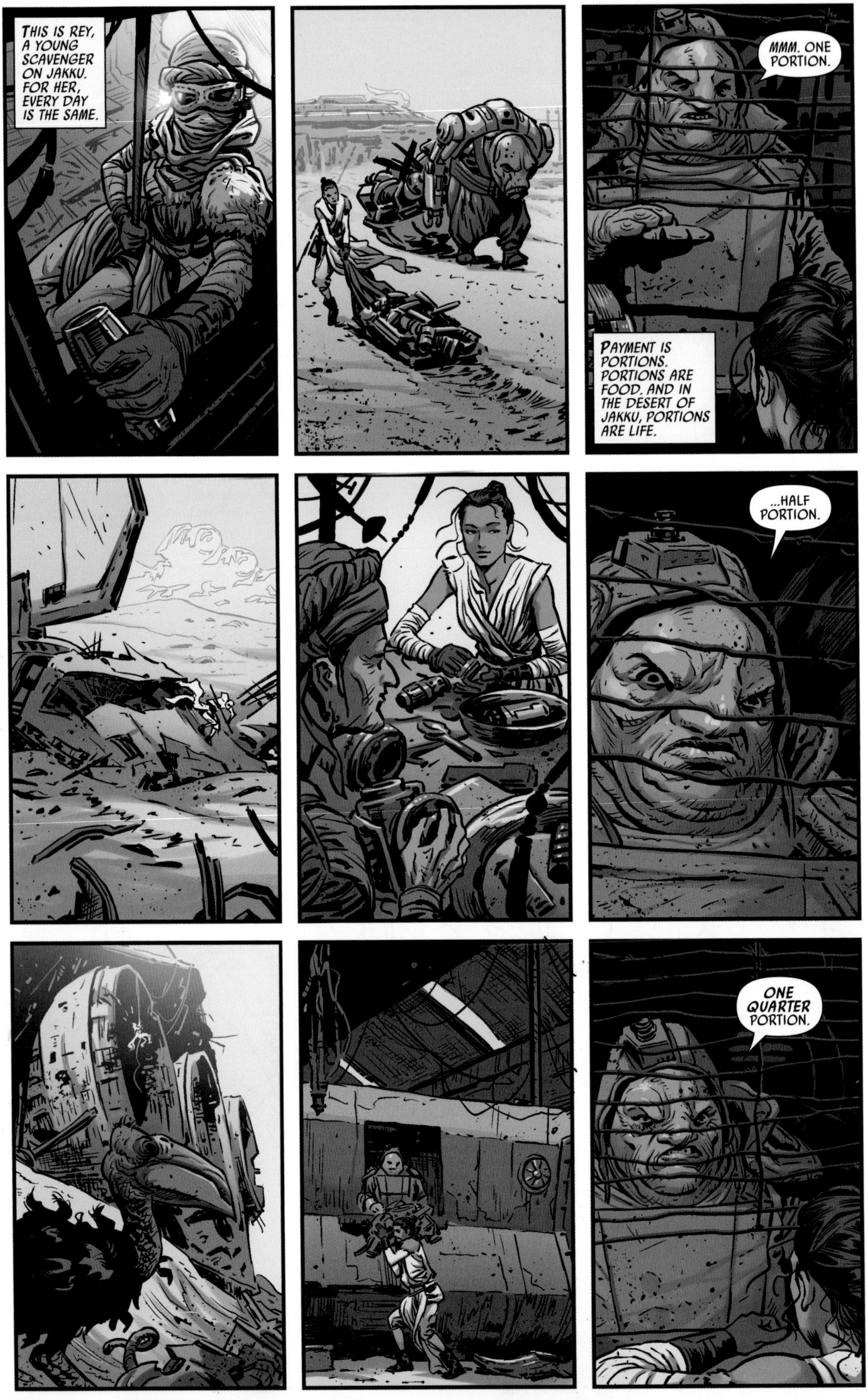
THIS IS REY, A YOUNG SCAVENGER ON JAKKU. FOR HER, EVERY DAY IS THE SAME.
MMM. ONE PORTION.
PAYMENT IS PORTIONS. PORTIONS ARE FOOD. AND IN THE DESERT OF JAKKU, PORTIONS ARE LIFE.
...HALF PORTION.
ONE QUARTER PORTION.

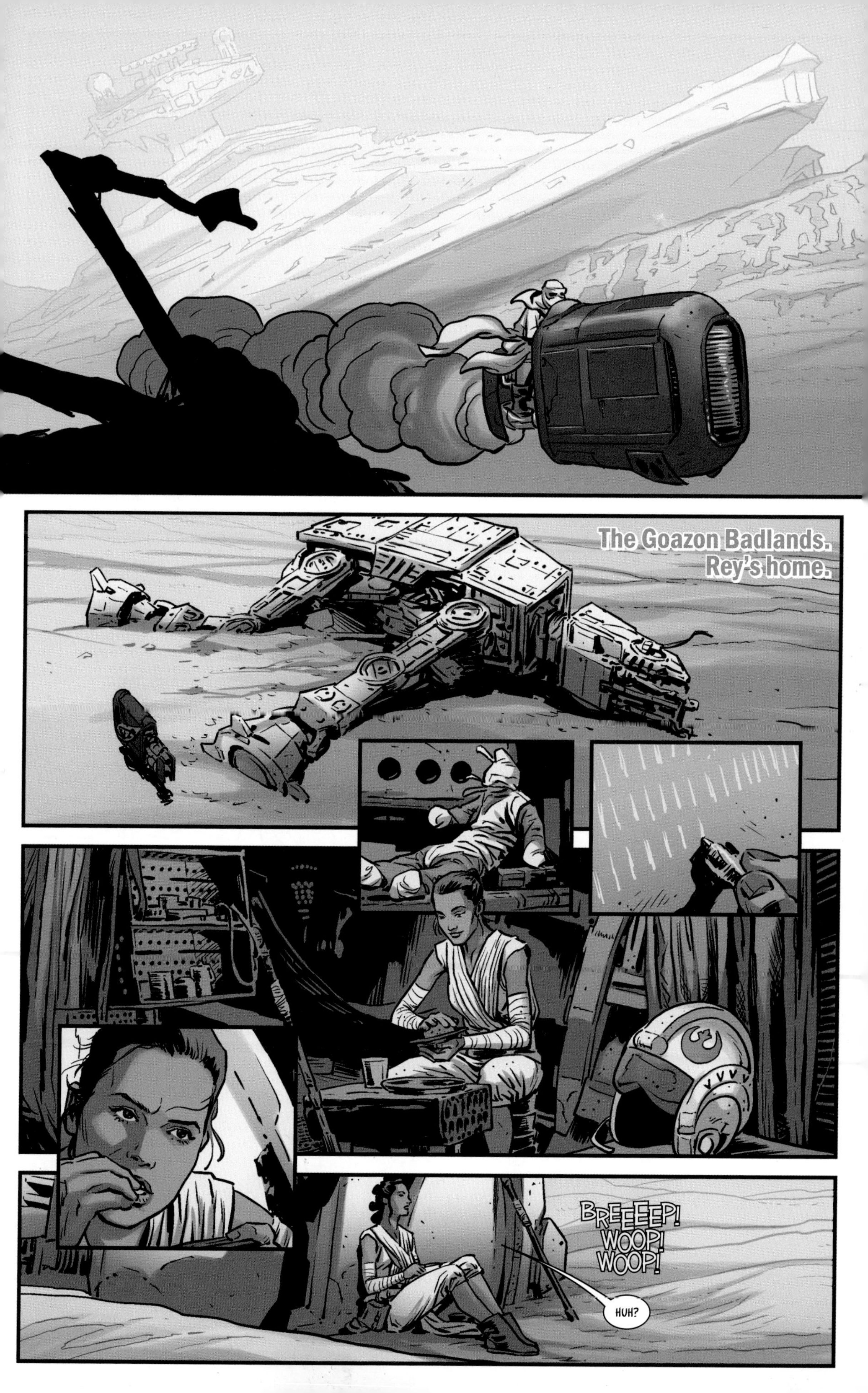
The Goazon Badlands.
Rey's home.
BREEEEP! WOOP! WOOP!
HUH?

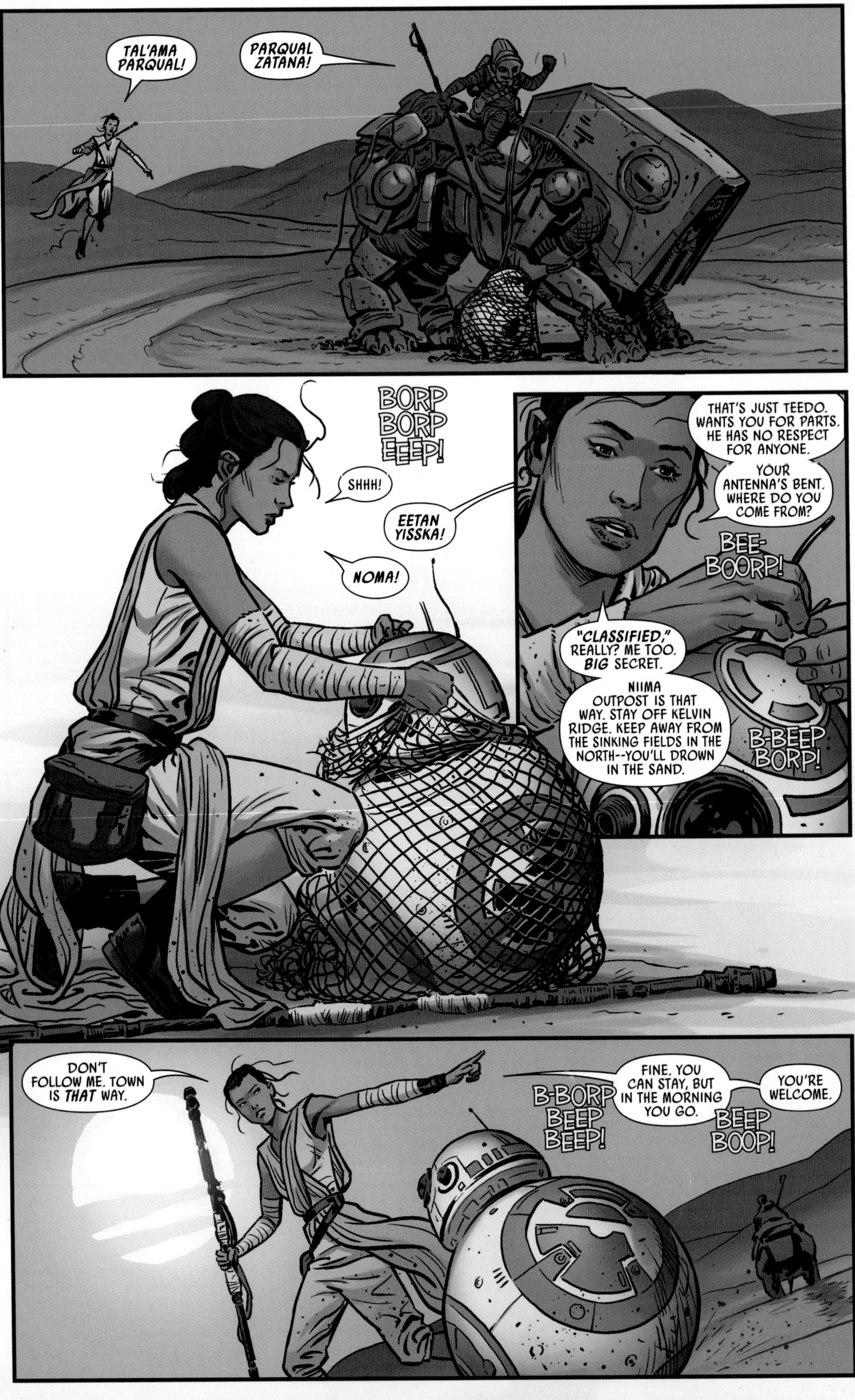
TAL'AMA PARQUAL!
PARQUAL ZATANA!
BORP BORP EEEEP!
SHHH!
EETAN YISSKA!
NOMA!
THAT'S JUST TEEDO. WANTS YOU FOR PARTS. HE HAS NO RESPECT FOR ANYONE.
YOUR ANTENNA'S BENT. WHERE DO YOU COME FROM?
BEE-BOORP!
"CLASSIFIED," REALLY? ME TOO. BIG SECRET.
NIIMA OUTPOST IS THAT WAY. STAY OFF KELVIN RIDGE. KEEP AWAY FROM THE SINKING FIELDS IN THE NORTH--YOU'LL DROWN IN THE SAND.
B-BEEP BORP!
DON'T FOLLOW ME. TOWN IS THAT WAY.
B-BORP BEEP BEEP!
FINE. YOU CAN STAY, BUT IN THE MORNING YOU GO.
BEEP BOOP!
YOU'RE WELCOME.

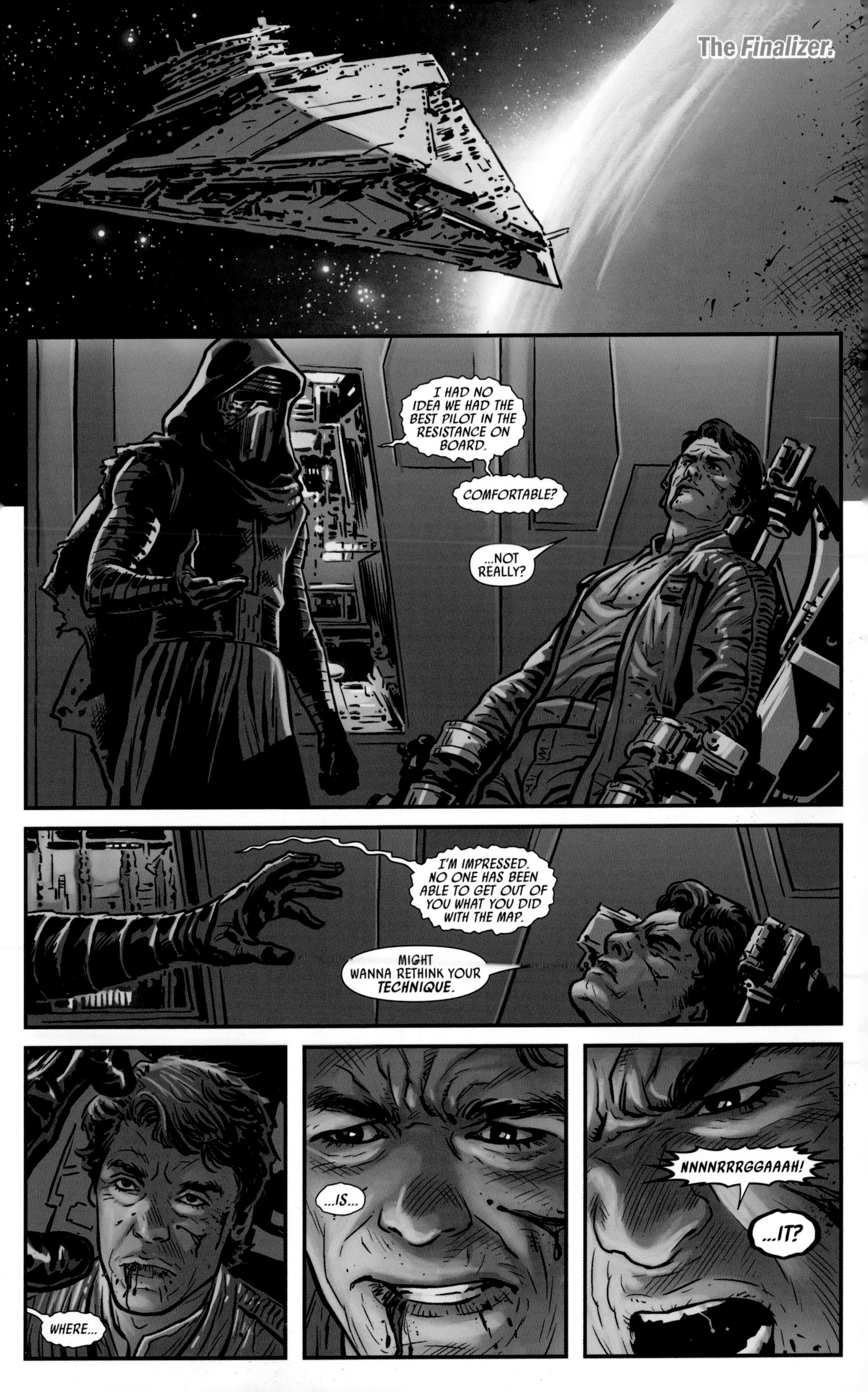
The Finalizer.
I HAD NO IDEA WE HAD THE BEST PILOT IN THE RESISTANCE ON BOARD.
COMFORTABLE?
...NOT REALLY?
I'M IMPRESSED. NO ONE HAS BEEN ABLE TO GET OUT OF YOU WHAT YOU DID WITH THE MAP.
MIGHT WANNA RETHINK YOUR TECHNIQUE.
WHERE...
...IS...
NNNNRRRGGAAAH!
...IT?

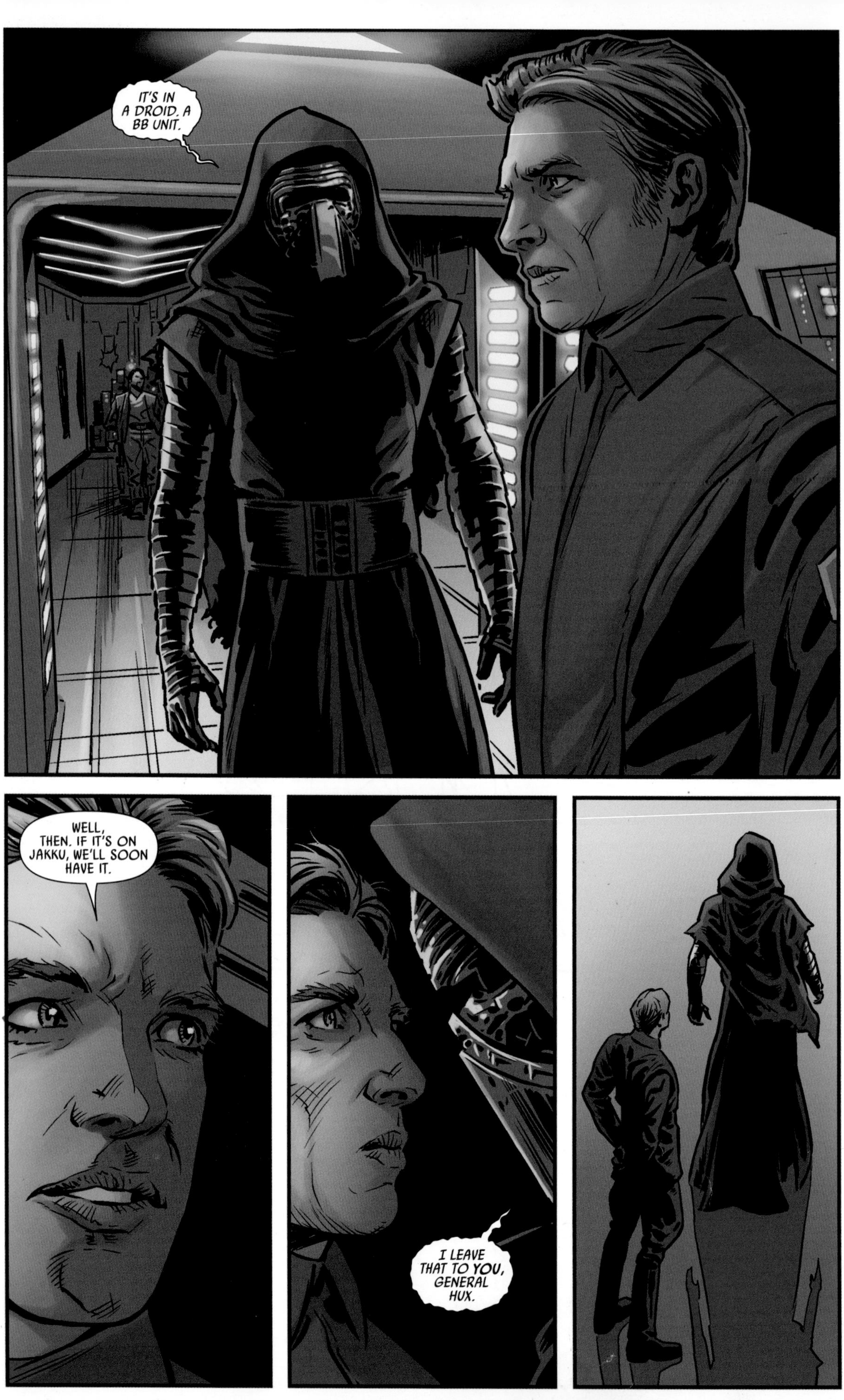
IT'S IN A DROID. A BB UNIT.
WELL, THEN. IF IT'S ON JAKKU, WE'LL SOON HAVE IT.
I LEAVE THAT TO YOU, GENERAL HUX.

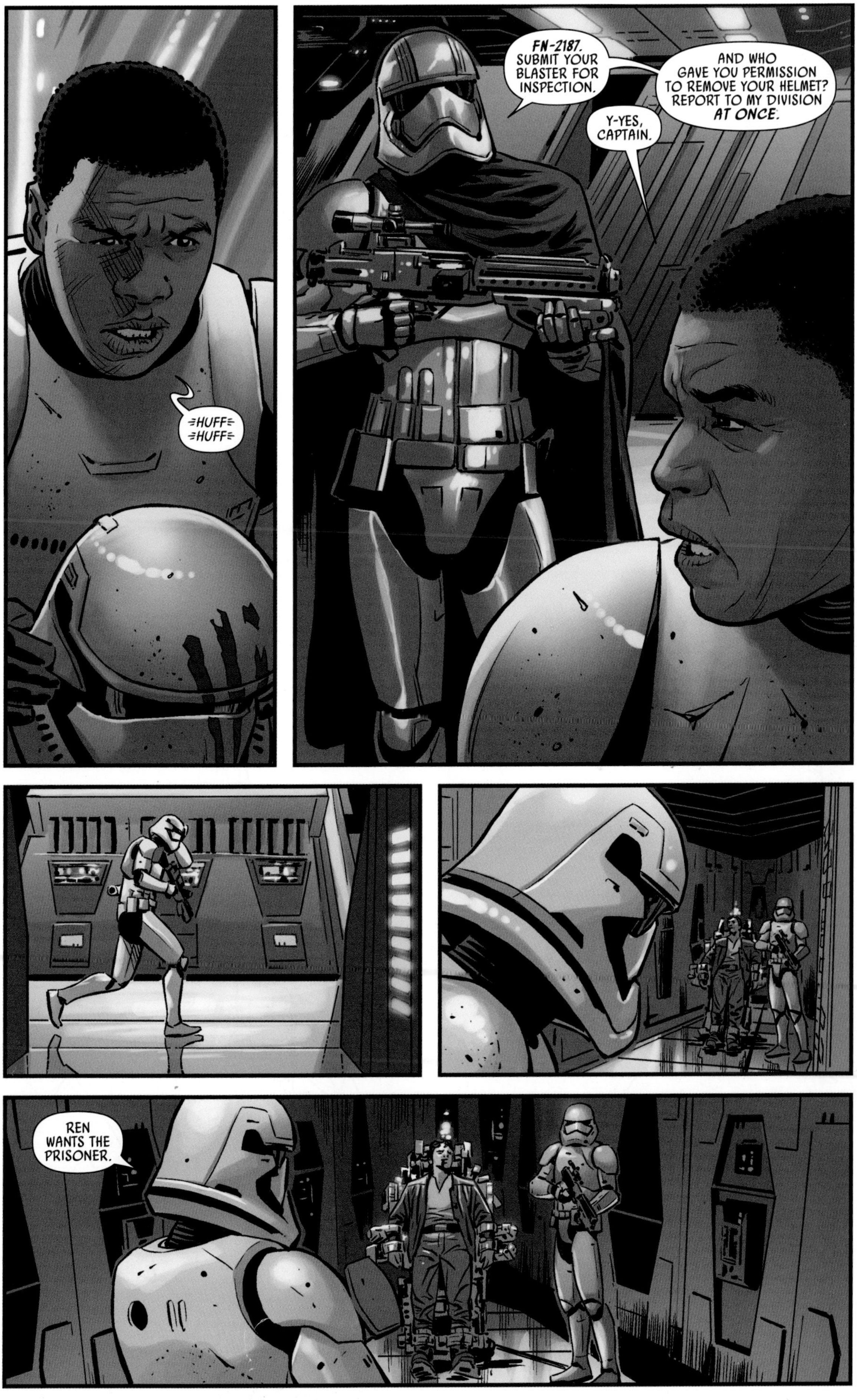

HUFF HUFF
FN-2187. SUBMIT YOUR BLASTER FOR INSPECTION.
AND WHO GAVE YOU PERMISSION TO REMOVE YOUR HELMET? REPORT TO MY DIVISION AT ONCE.
Y-YES, CAPTAIN.
REN WANTS THE PRISONER.

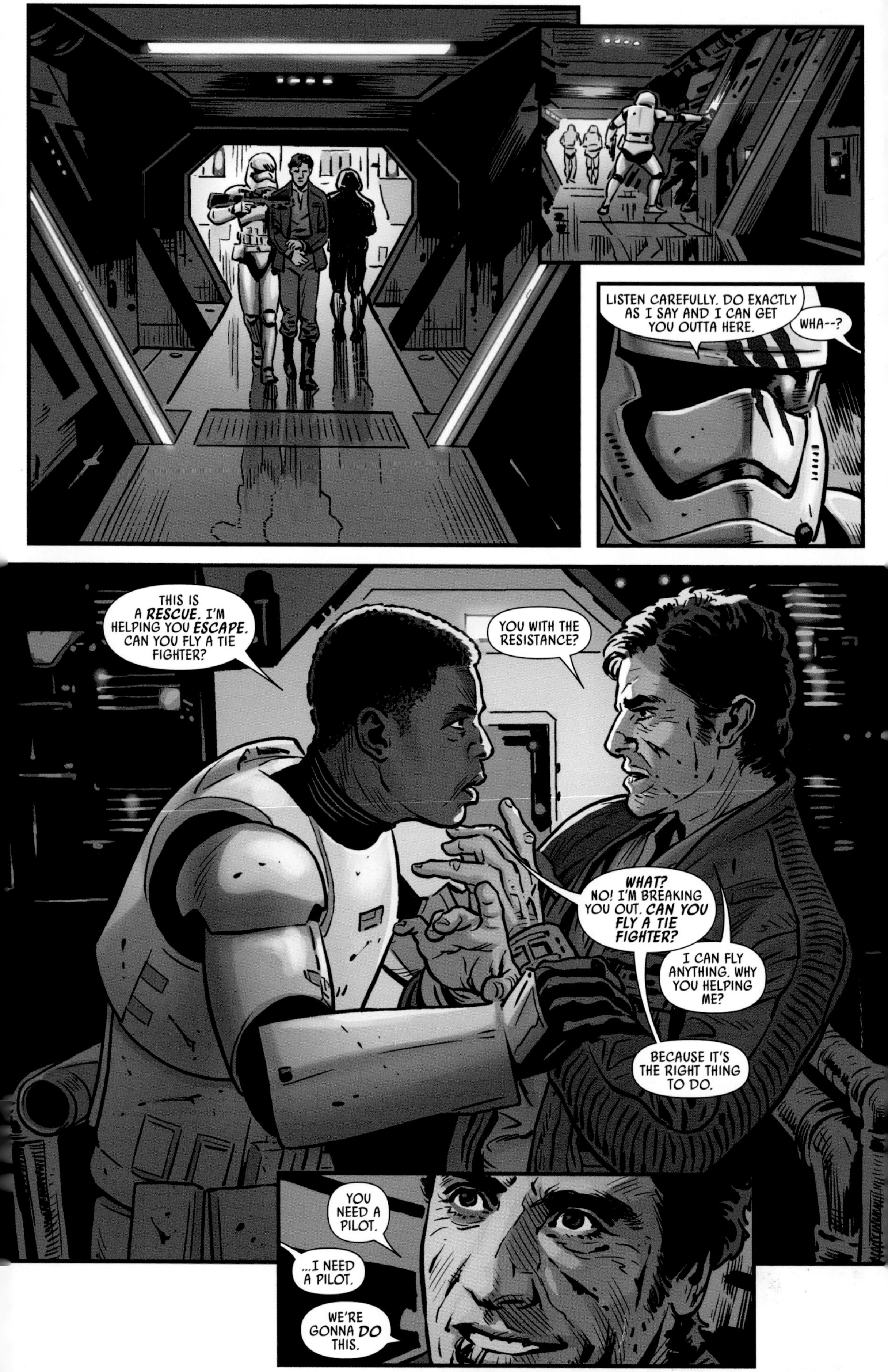
LISTEN CAREFULLY. DO EXACTLY AS I SAY AND I CAN GET YOU OUTTA HERE.
WHA--?
THIS IS A *RESCUE*. I'M HELPING YOU *ESCAPE*. CAN YOU FLY A TIE FIGHTER?
YOU WITH THE RESISTANCE?
WHAT? NO! I'M BREAKING YOU OUT. *CAN YOU FLY A TIE FIGHTER?*
I CAN FLY ANYTHING. WHY YOU HELPING ME?
BECAUSE IT'S THE RIGHT THING TO DO.
YOU NEED A PILOT.
...I NEED A PILOT.
WE'RE GONNA *DO* THIS.

STAY CALM. STAY CALM.
I'M TALKING TO MYSELF.
I AM CALM.
OKAY, GO. THIS WAY!
ALL RIGHT? EVERYBODY COMFORTABLE?
I ALWAYS WANTED TO FLY ONE OF THESE THINGS. CAN YOU SHOOT?
BLASTERS, I CAN.
SAME PRINCIPLE. TOGGLE ON LEFT TO SWITCH BETWEEN MISSILES, CANNONS, MAG PULSE. SIGHTS ON THE RIGHT TO AIM. TRIGGERS TO FIRE.
...THIS IS VERY COMPLICATED.

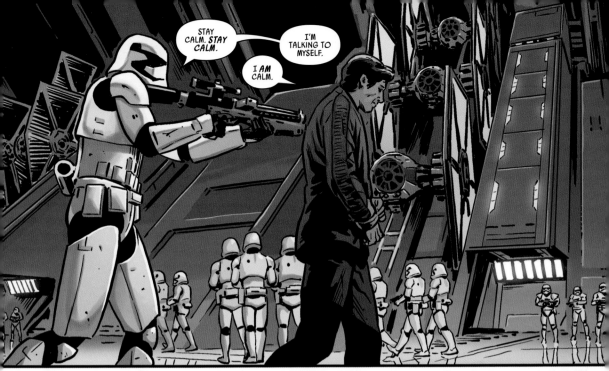

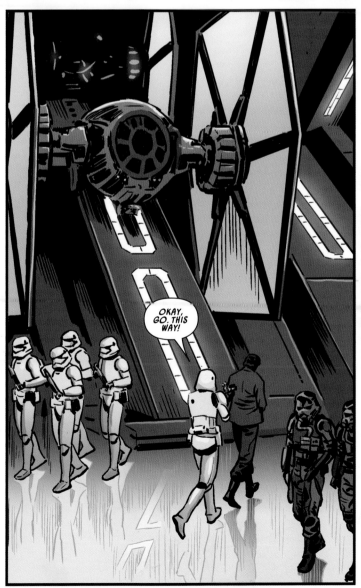

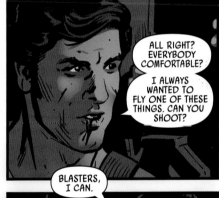

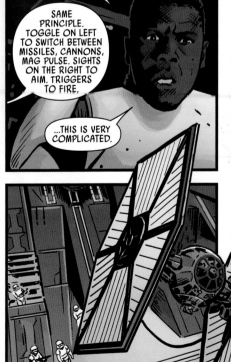

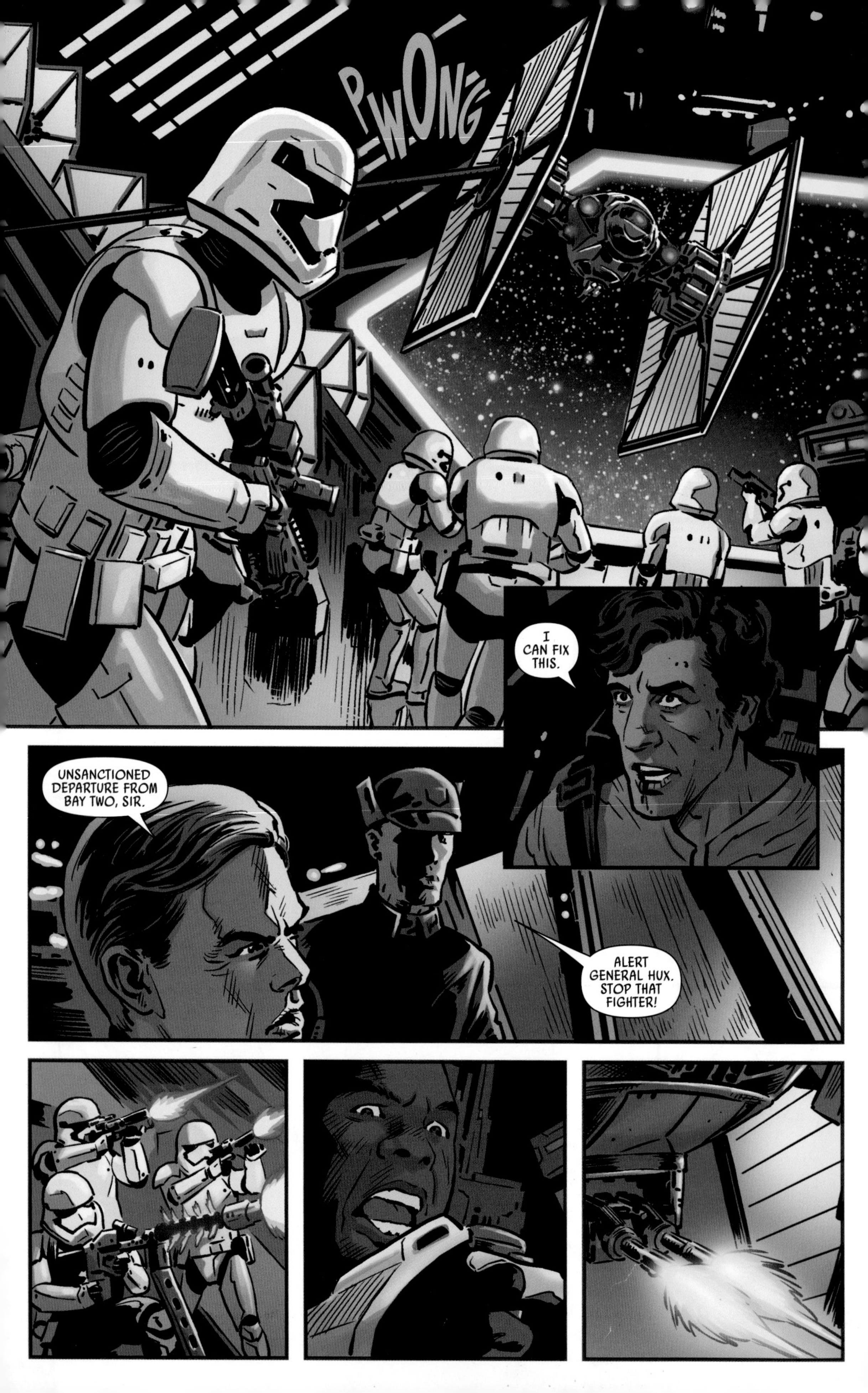
PWONG
I CAN FIX THIS.
UNSANCTIONED DEPARTURE FROM BAY TWO, SIR.
ALERT GENERAL HUX. STOP THAT FIGHTER!

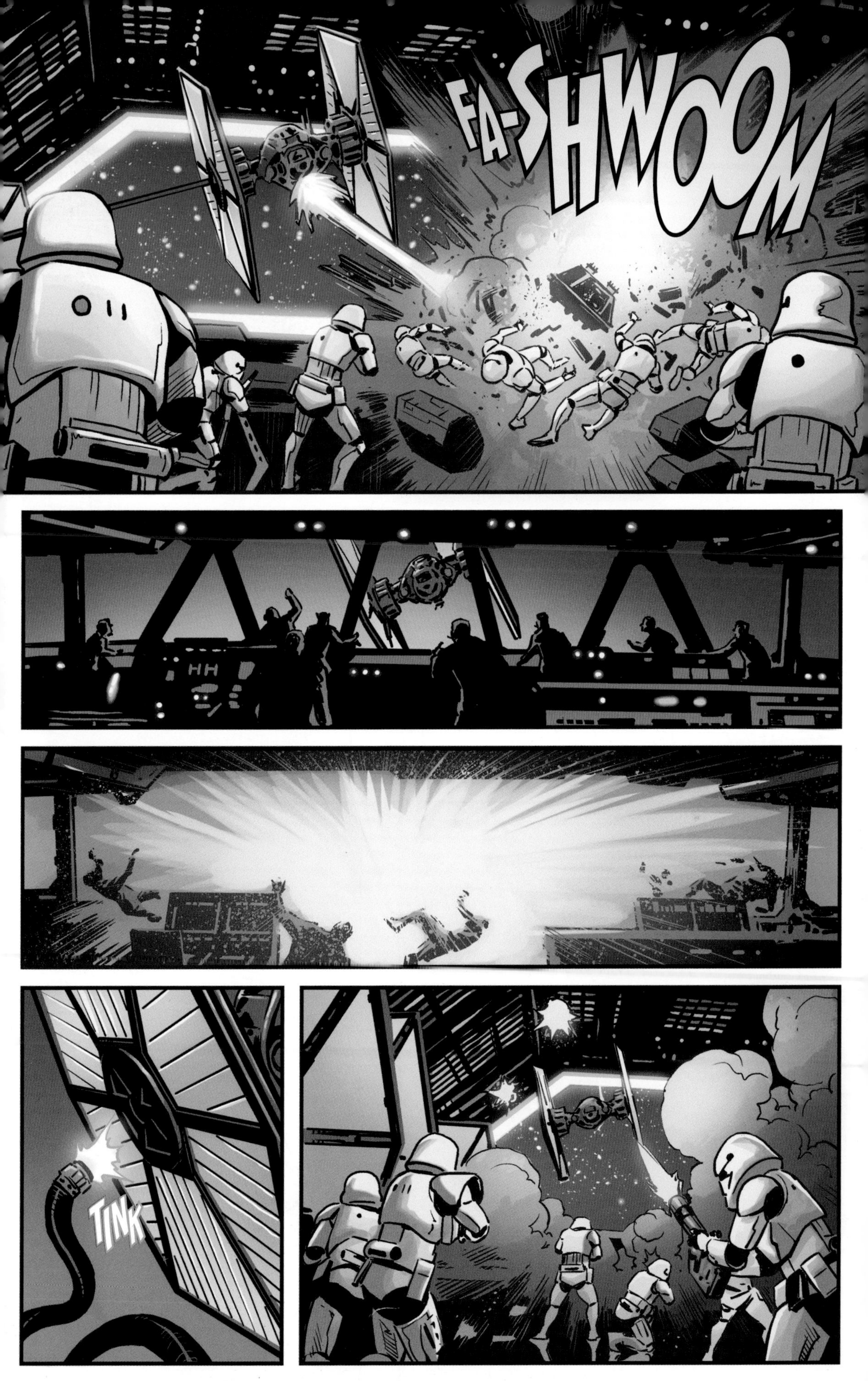
FA-SHWOOM
TINK

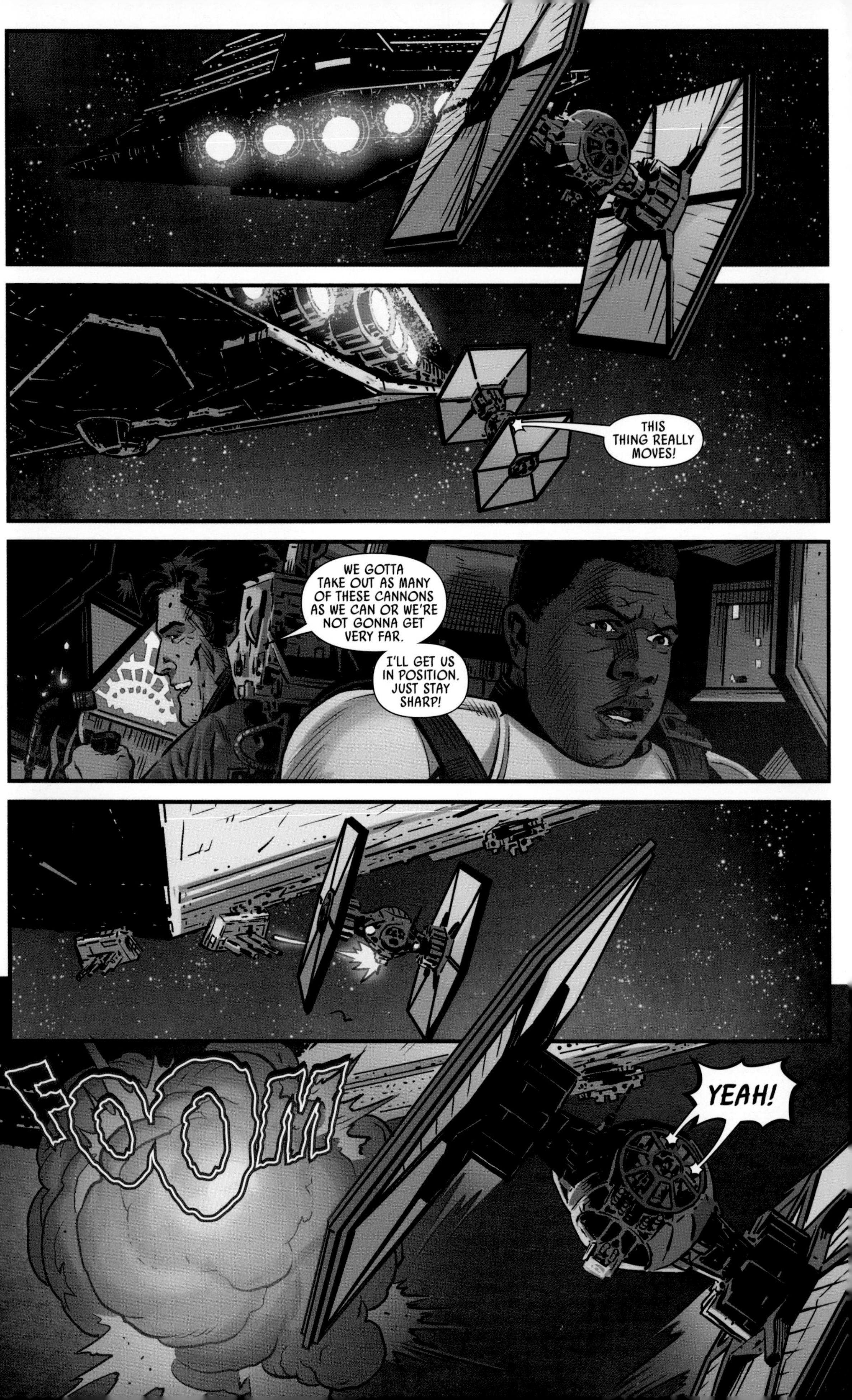
THIS THING REALLY MOVES!
WE GOTTA TAKE OUT AS MANY OF THESE CANNONS AS WE CAN OR WE'RE NOT GONNA GET VERY FAR.
I'LL GET US IN POSITION. JUST STAY SHARP!
FOOM
YEAH!

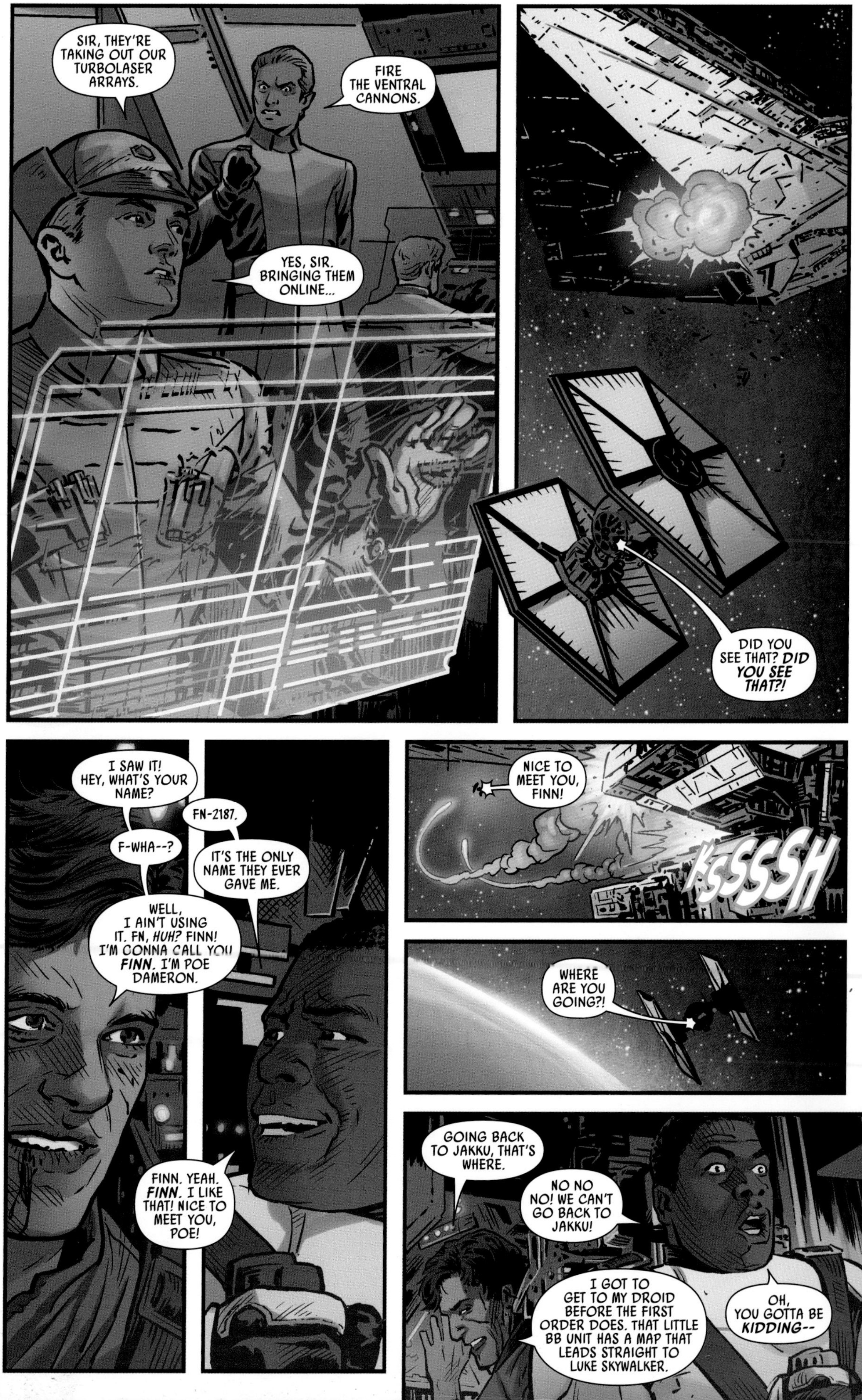
SIR, THEY'RE TAKING OUT OUR TURBOLASER ARRAYS.
FIRE THE VENTRAL CANNONS.
YES, SIR. BRINGING THEM ONLINE...
DID YOU SEE THAT? *DID YOU SEE THAT?!*
I SAW IT! HEY, WHAT'S YOUR NAME?
FN-2187.
F-WHA--?
IT'S THE ONLY NAME THEY EVER GAVE ME.
WELL, I AIN'T USING IT. FN, *HUH?* FINN! I'M GONNA CALL YOU *FINN.* I'M POE DAMERON.
FINN. YEAH. *FINN.* I LIKE THAT! NICE TO MEET YOU, POE!
NICE TO MEET YOU, FINN!
KSSSSH
WHERE ARE YOU GOING?!
GOING BACK TO JAKKU, THAT'S WHERE.
NO NO NO! WE CAN'T GO BACK TO JAKKU!
I GOT TO GET TO MY DROID BEFORE THE FIRST ORDER DOES. THAT LITTLE BB UNIT HAS A MAP THAT LEADS STRAIGHT TO LUKE SKYWALKER.
OH, YOU GOTTA BE *KIDDING--*

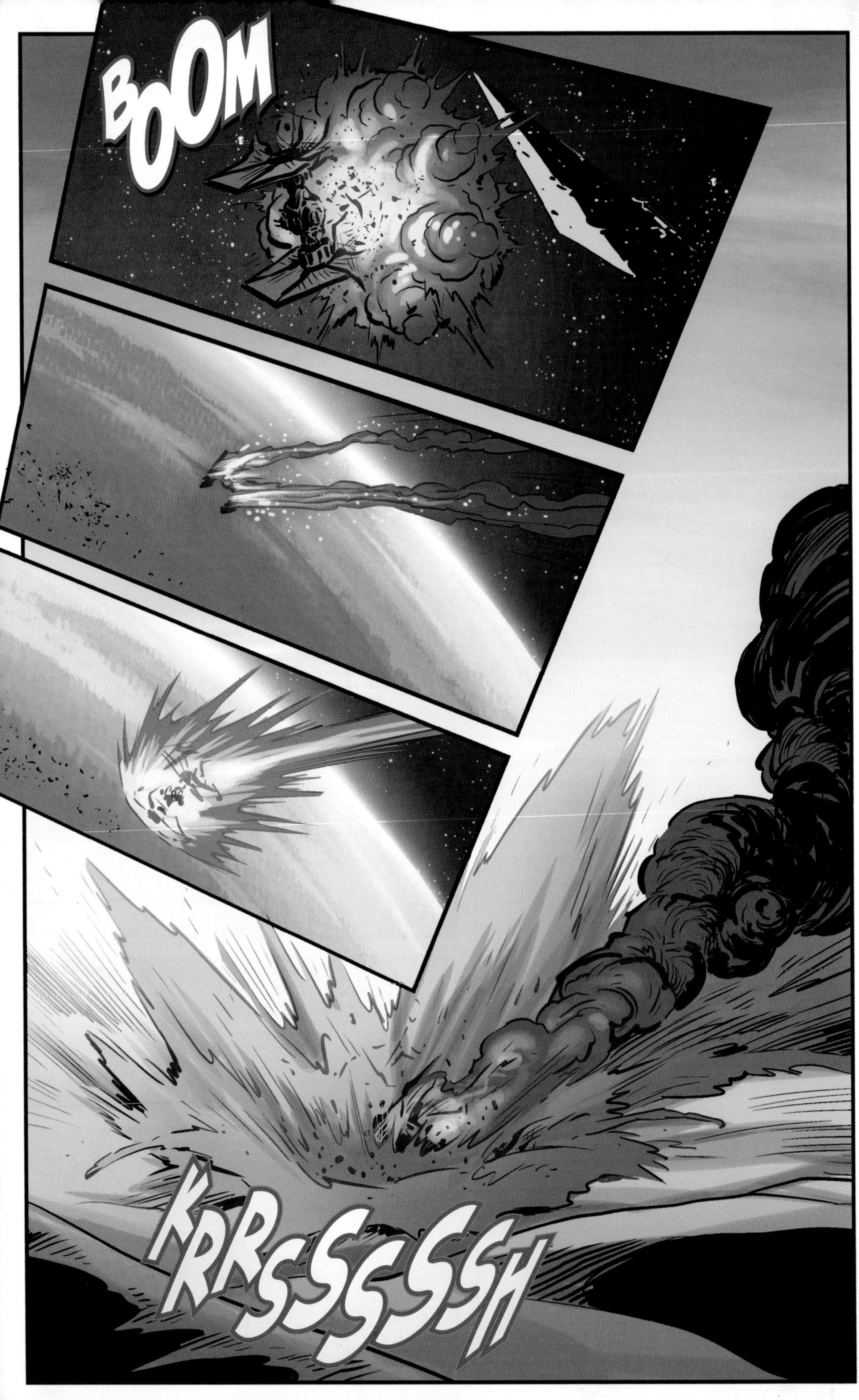
BOOM
KRRSSSSSH

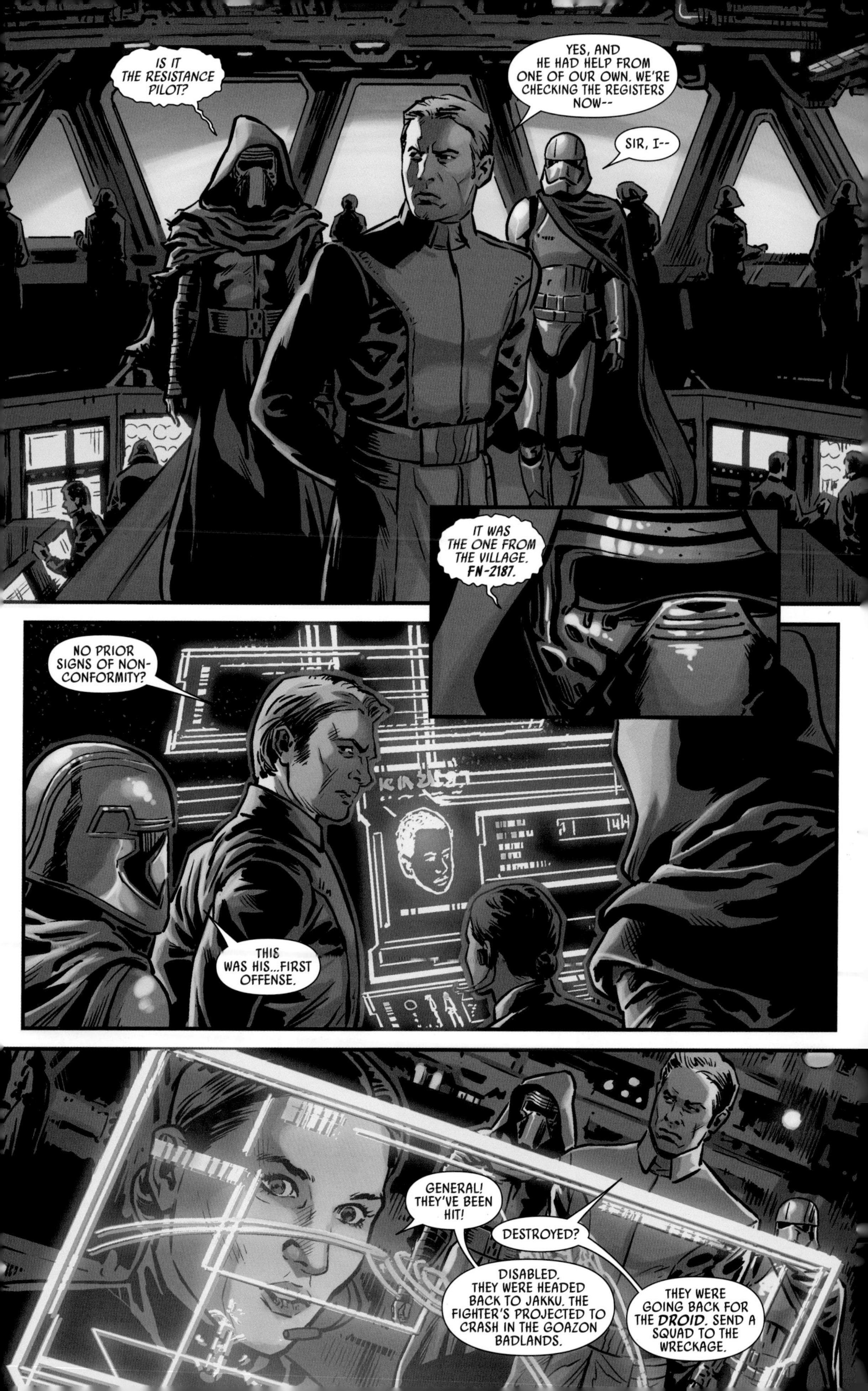
IS IT THE RESISTANCE PILOT?
YES, AND HE HAD HELP FROM ONE OF OUR OWN. WE'RE CHECKING THE REGISTERS NOW--
SIR, I--
IT WAS THE ONE FROM THE VILLAGE. FN-2187.
NO PRIOR SIGNS OF NON-CONFORMITY?
THIS WAS HIS...FIRST OFFENSE.
GENERAL! THEY'VE BEEN HIT!
DESTROYED?
DISABLED. THEY WERE HEADED BACK TO JAKKU. THE FIGHTER'S PROJECTED TO CRASH IN THE GOAZON BADLANDS.
THEY WERE GOING BACK FOR THE DROID. SEND A SQUAD TO THE WRECKAGE.

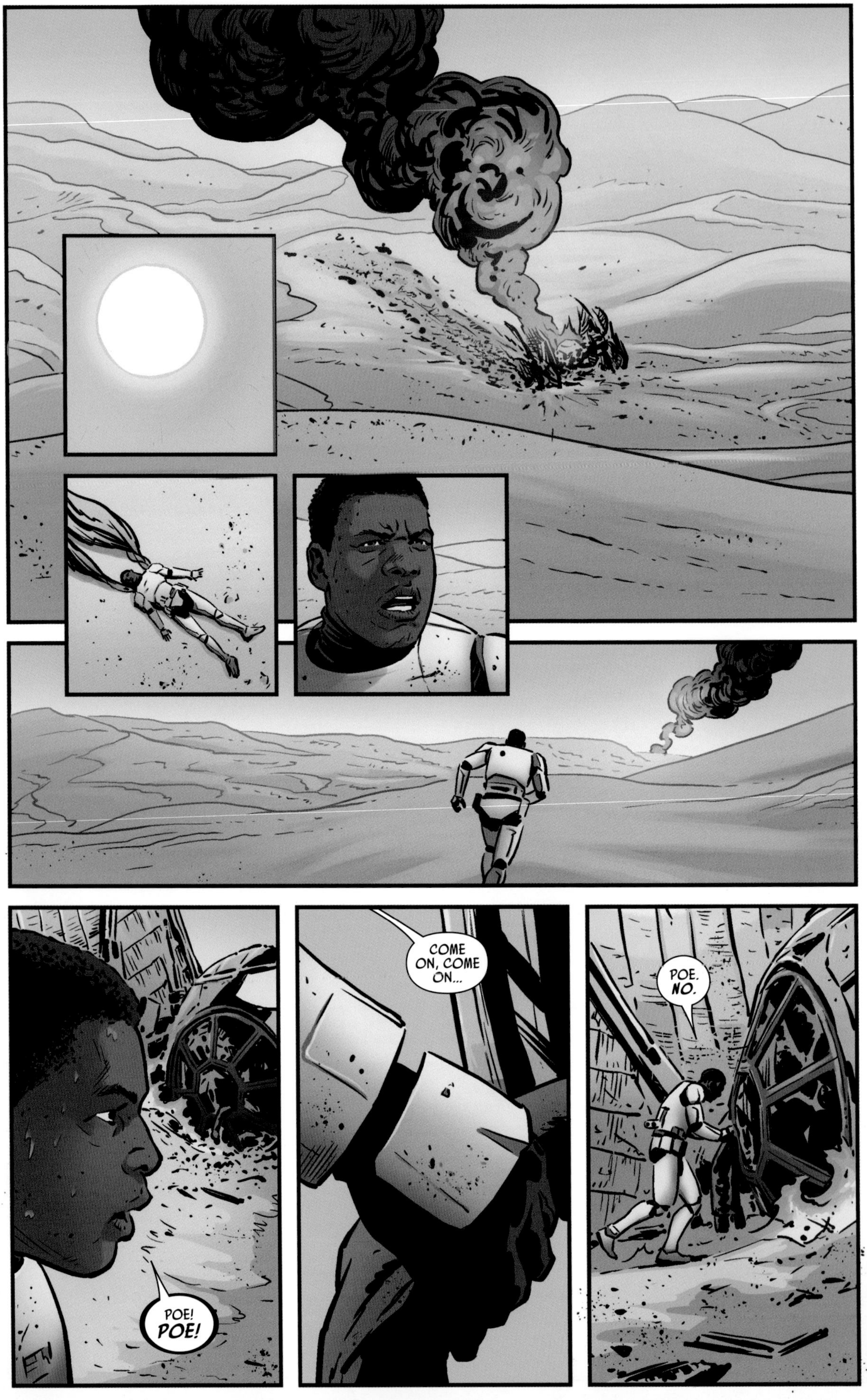
POE! POE!
COME ON, COME ON...
POE. NO.

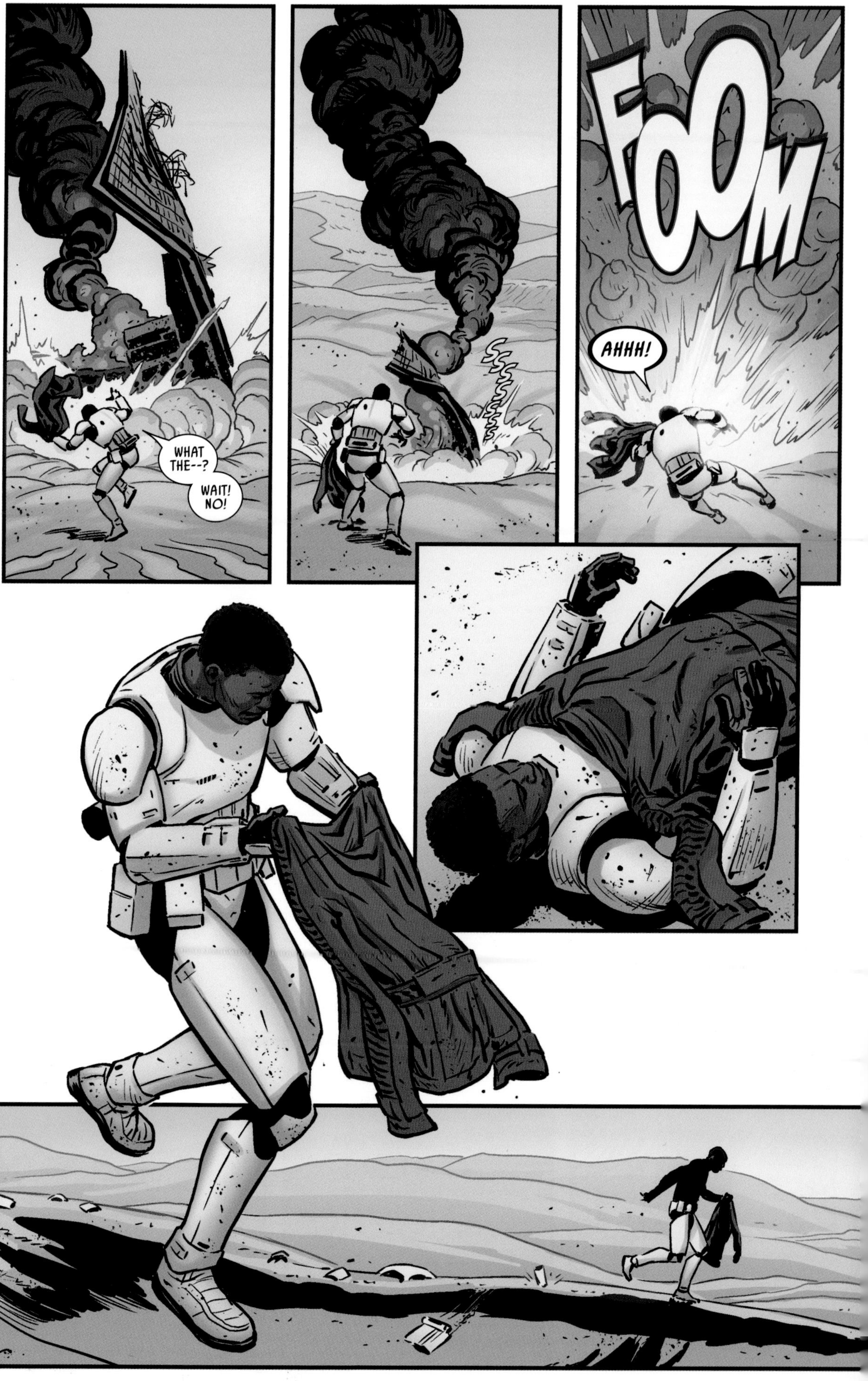
WHAT THE--?
WAIT! NO!
SSSSSSSSS
FOOM
AHHH!

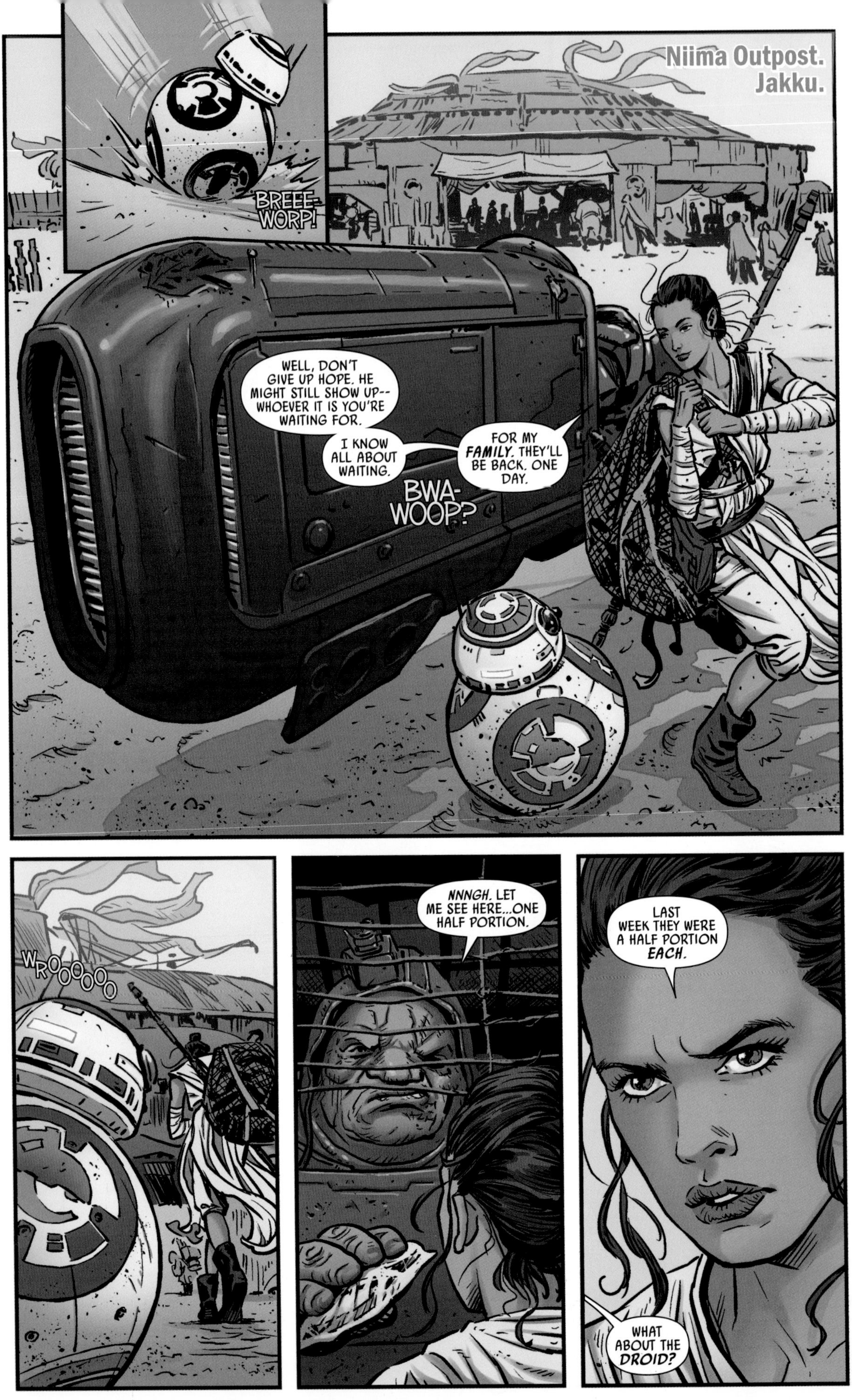
BREEE-WORP!
Niima Outpost. Jakku.
WELL, DON'T GIVE UP HOPE. HE MIGHT STILL SHOW UP--WHOEVER IT IS YOU'RE WAITING FOR.
I KNOW ALL ABOUT WAITING.
FOR MY FAMILY. THEY'LL BE BACK, ONE DAY.
BWA-WOOP?
WROOOOOO
NNNGH. LET ME SEE HERE...ONE HALF PORTION.
LAST WEEK THEY WERE A HALF PORTION EACH.
WHAT ABOUT THE DROID?

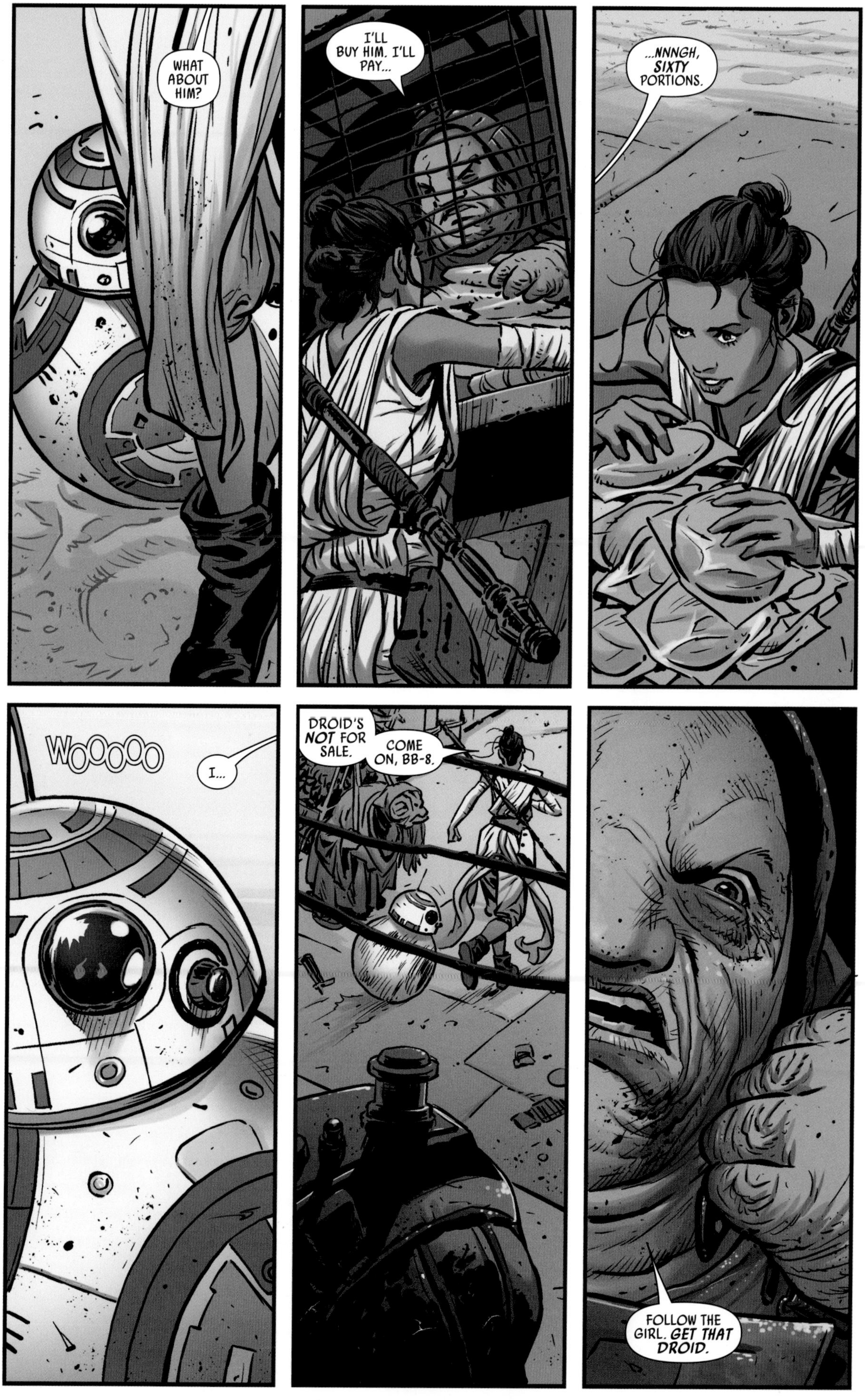
WHAT ABOUT HIM?
I'LL BUY HIM. I'LL PAY...
...NNNGH, SIXTY PORTIONS.
WOOOOO
I...
DROID'S NOT FOR SALE.
COME ON, BB-8.
FOLLOW THE GIRL. GET THAT DROID.

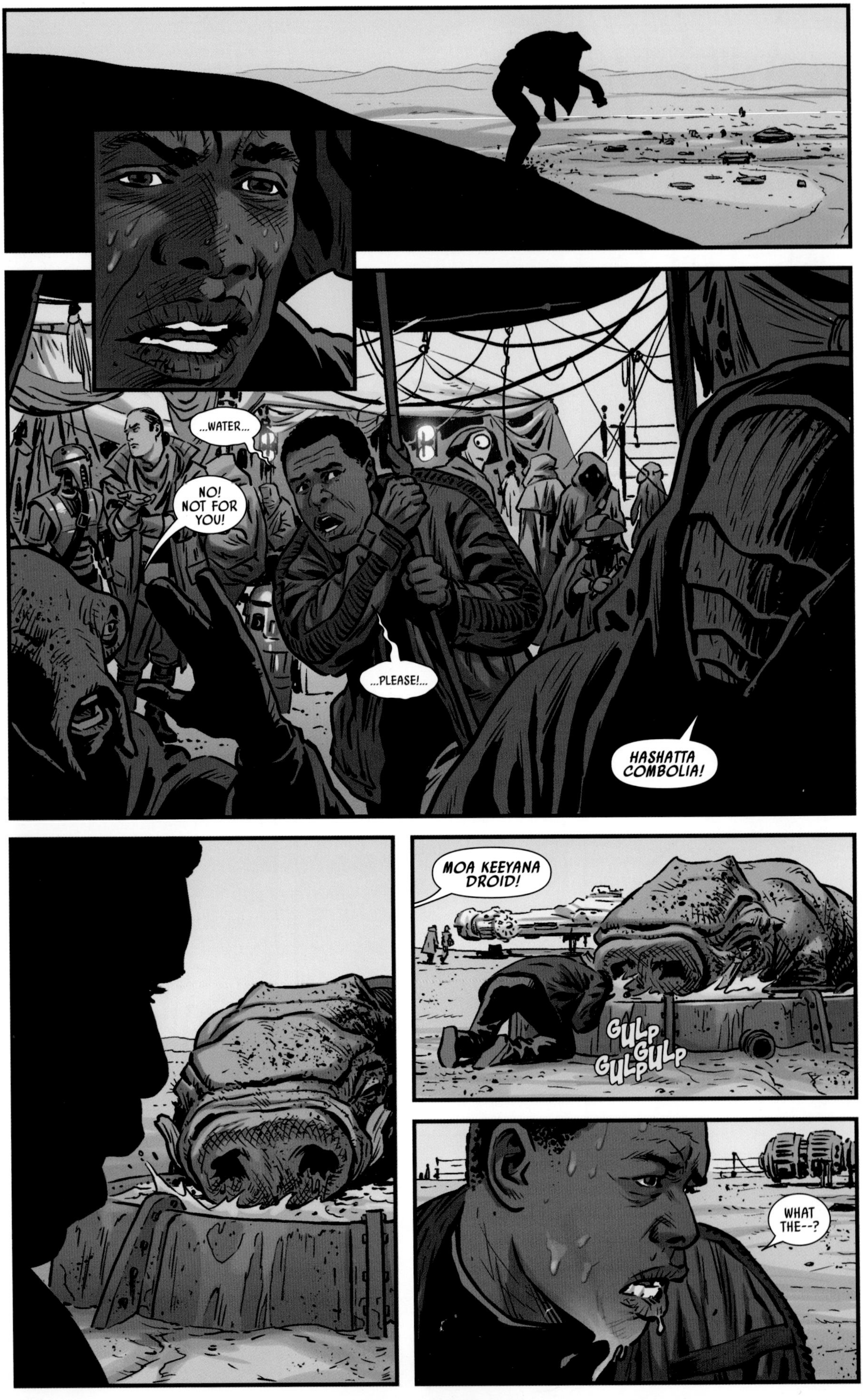
...WATER...
NO! NOT FOR YOU!
...PLEASE!...
HASHATTA COMBOLIA!
MOA KEEYANA DROID!
GULP GULP GULP
WHAT THE--?

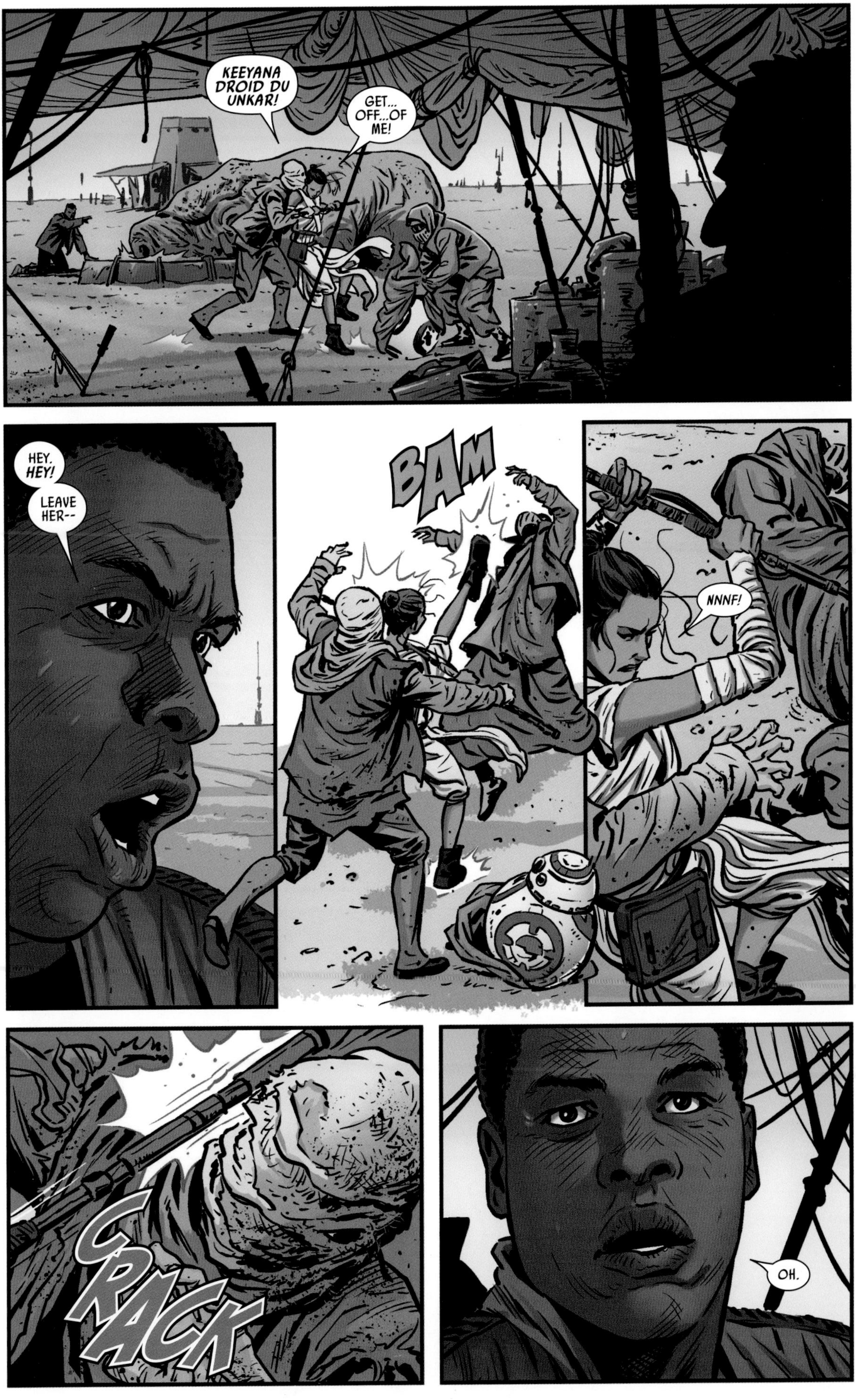
KEEYANA DROID DU UNKAR!
GET... OFF...OF ME!
HEY. HEY!
LEAVE HER--
BAM
NNNF!
CRACK
OH.

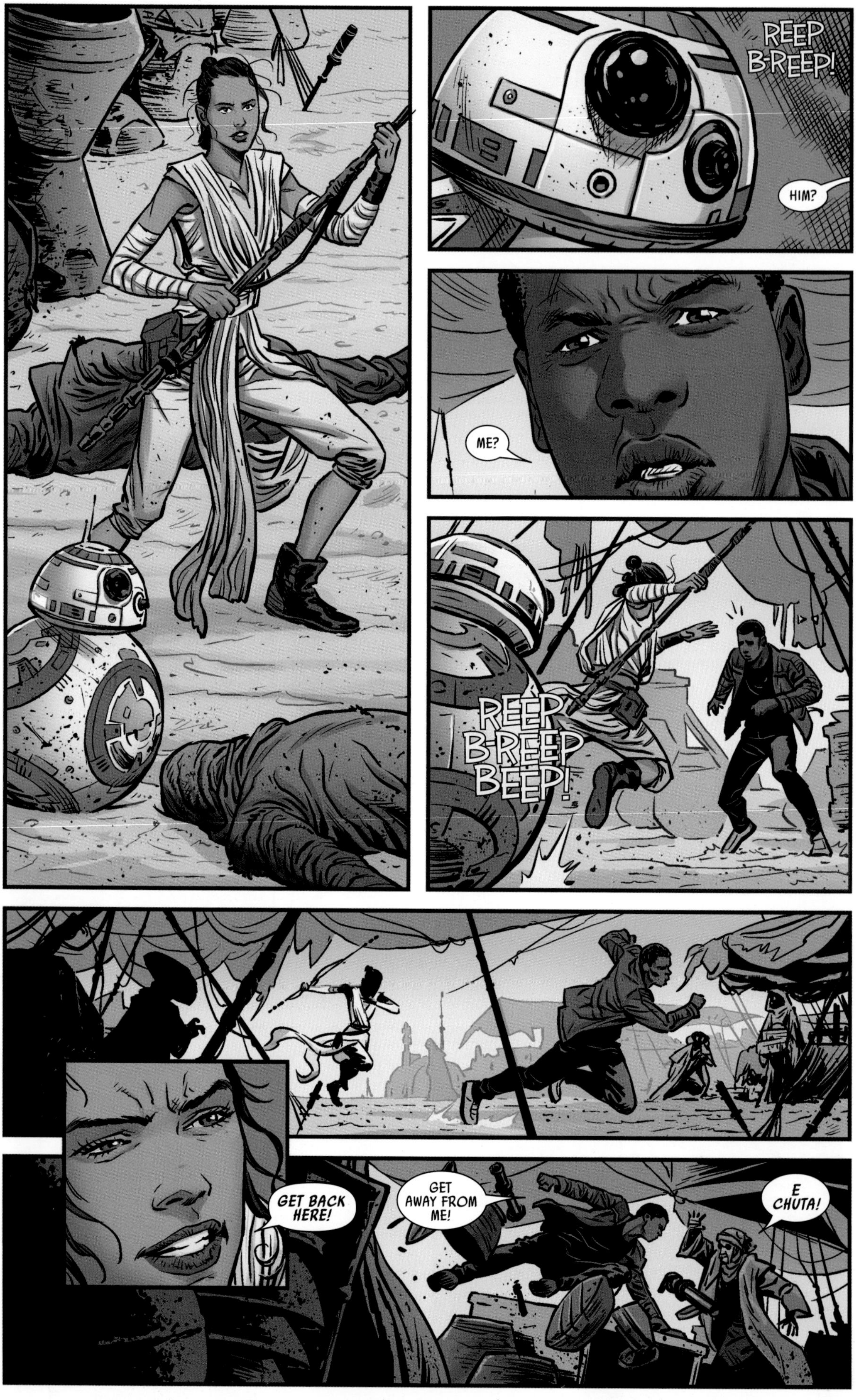
REEP B-REEP!
HIM?
ME?
REEP B-REEP BEEP!
GET BACK HERE!
GET AWAY FROM ME!
E CHUTA!

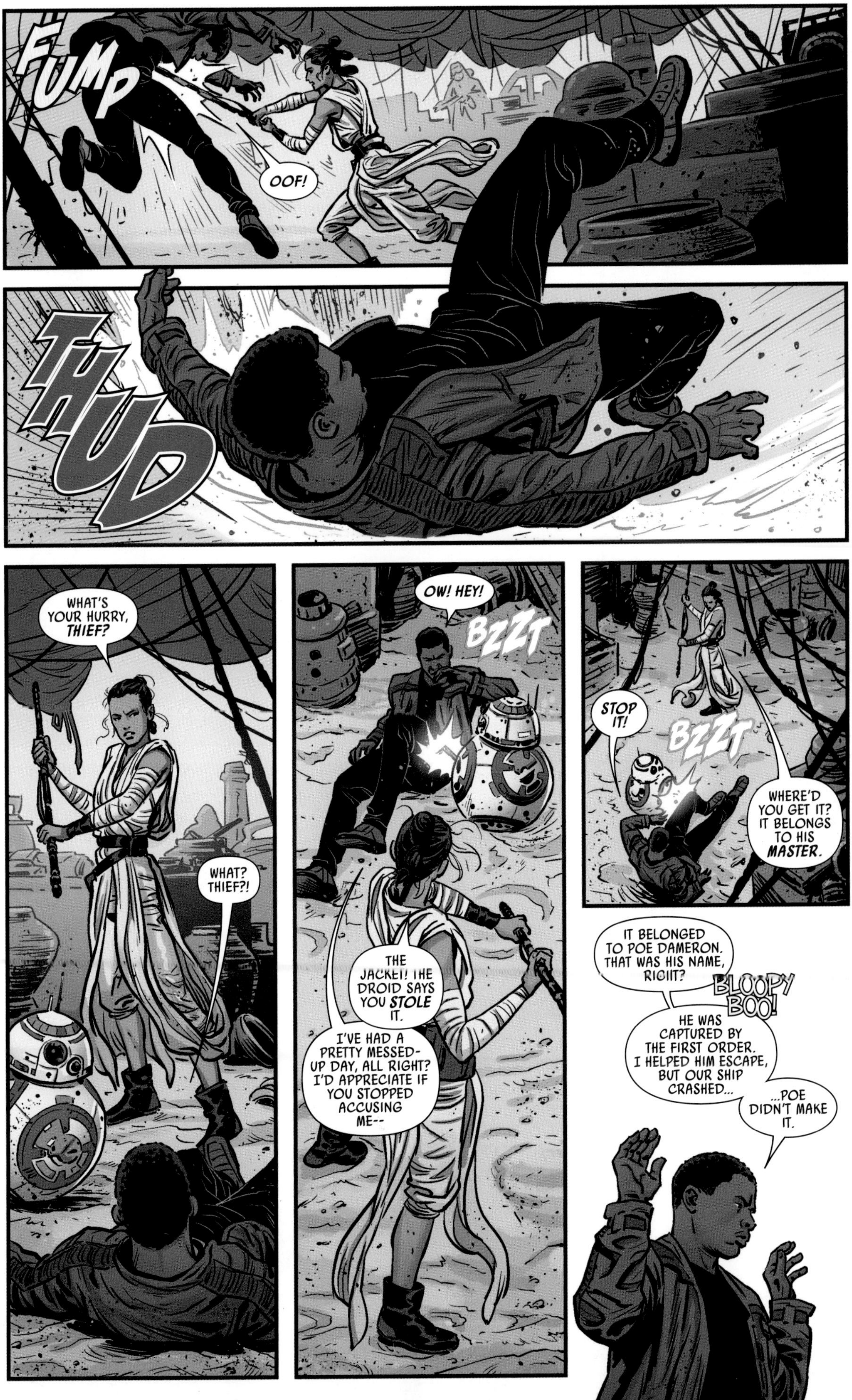
FUMP
OOF!
THUD
WHAT'S YOUR HURRY, THIEF?
WHAT? THIEF?!
OW! HEY!
BZZT
THE JACKET! THE DROID SAYS YOU STOLE IT.
I'VE HAD A PRETTY MESSED-UP DAY, ALL RIGHT? I'D APPRECIATE IF YOU STOPPED ACCUSING ME--
STOP IT!
BZZT
WHERE'D YOU GET IT? IT BELONGS TO HIS MASTER.
IT BELONGED TO POE DAMERON. THAT WAS HIS NAME, RIGHT?
BLOOPY BOO!
HE WAS CAPTURED BY THE FIRST ORDER. I HELPED HIM ESCAPE, BUT OUR SHIP CRASHED...
...POE DIDN'T MAKE IT.

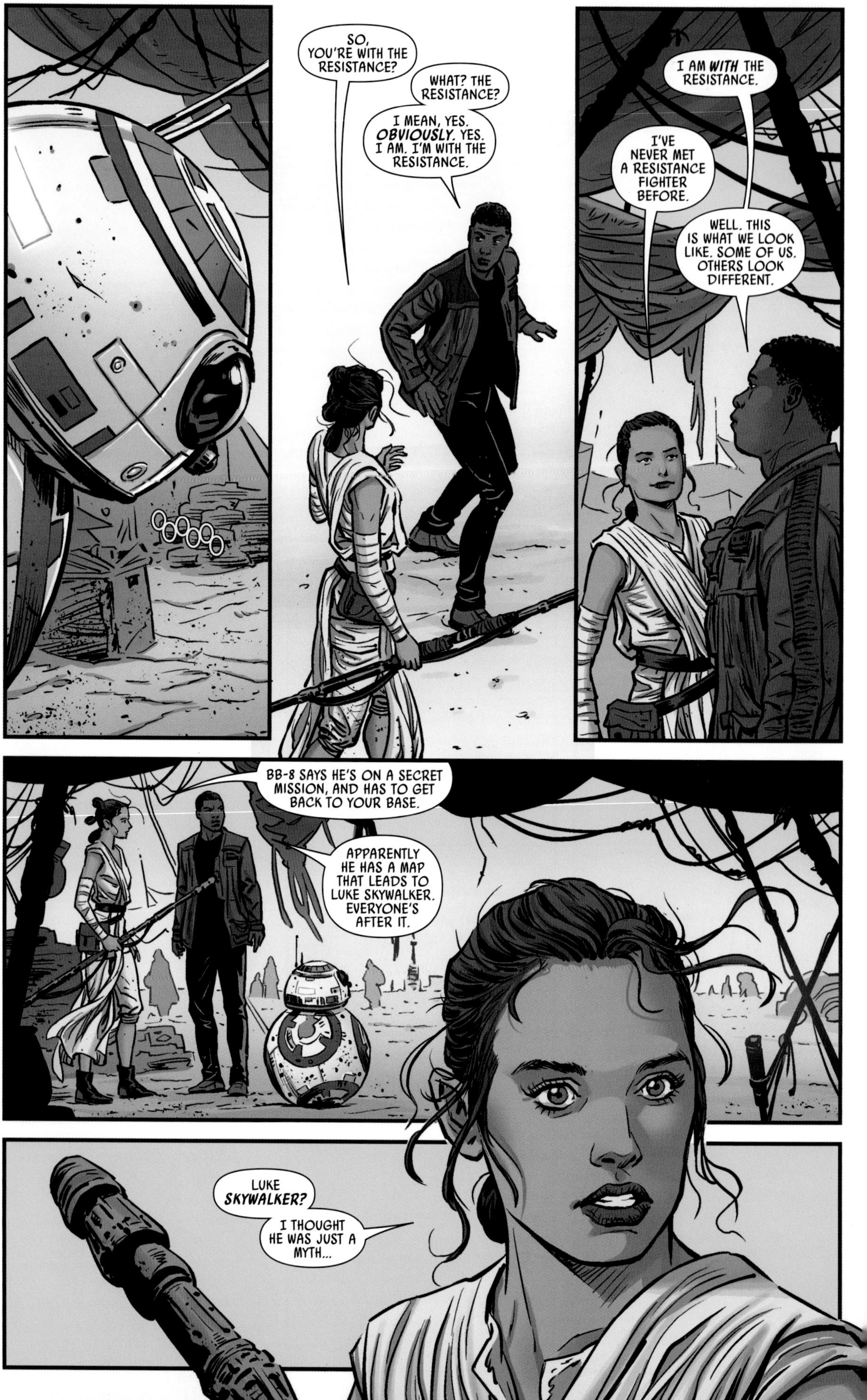
SO, YOU'RE WITH THE RESISTANCE?
WHAT? THE RESISTANCE?
I MEAN, YES. OBVIOUSLY. YES. I AM. I'M WITH THE RESISTANCE.
I AM WITH THE RESISTANCE.
I'VE NEVER MET A RESISTANCE FIGHTER BEFORE.
WELL. THIS IS WHAT WE LOOK LIKE. SOME OF US. OTHERS LOOK DIFFERENT.
BB-8 SAYS HE'S ON A SECRET MISSION, AND HAS TO GET BACK TO YOUR BASE.
APPARENTLY HE HAS A MAP THAT LEADS TO LUKE SKYWALKER. EVERYONE'S AFTER IT.
LUKE SKYWALKER?
I THOUGHT HE WAS JUST A MYTH...

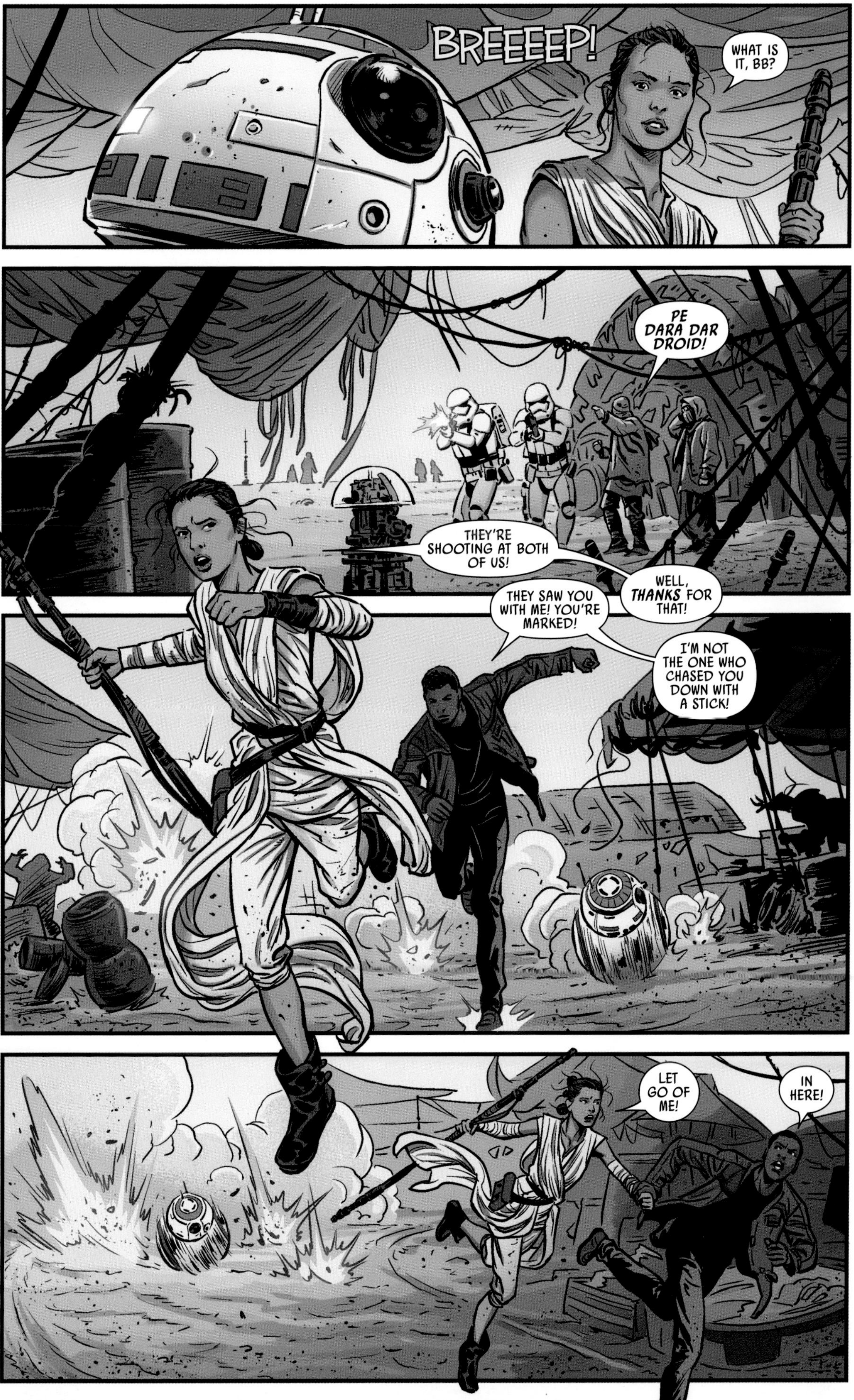
BREEEEP!
WHAT IS IT, BB?
PE DARA DAR DROID!
THEY'RE SHOOTING AT BOTH OF US!
WELL, THANKS FOR THAT!
THEY SAW YOU WITH ME! YOU'RE MARKED!
I'M NOT THE ONE WHO CHASED YOU DOWN WITH A STICK!
LET GO OF ME!
IN HERE!

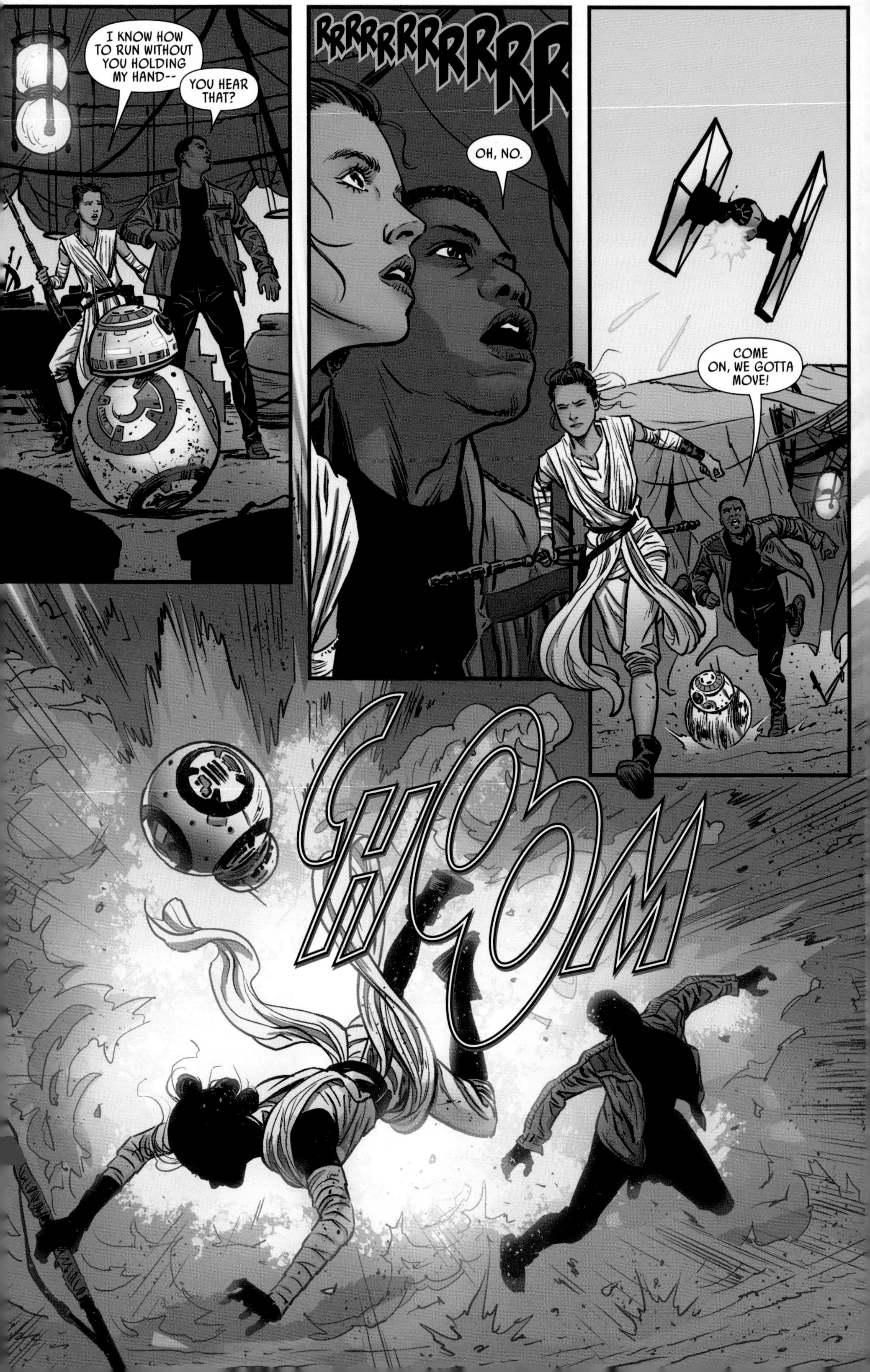
I KNOW HOW TO RUN WITHOUT YOU HOLDING MY HAND--
YOU HEAR THAT?
RRRRRRRRRR
OH, NO.
COME ON, WE GOTTA MOVE!
THOOM

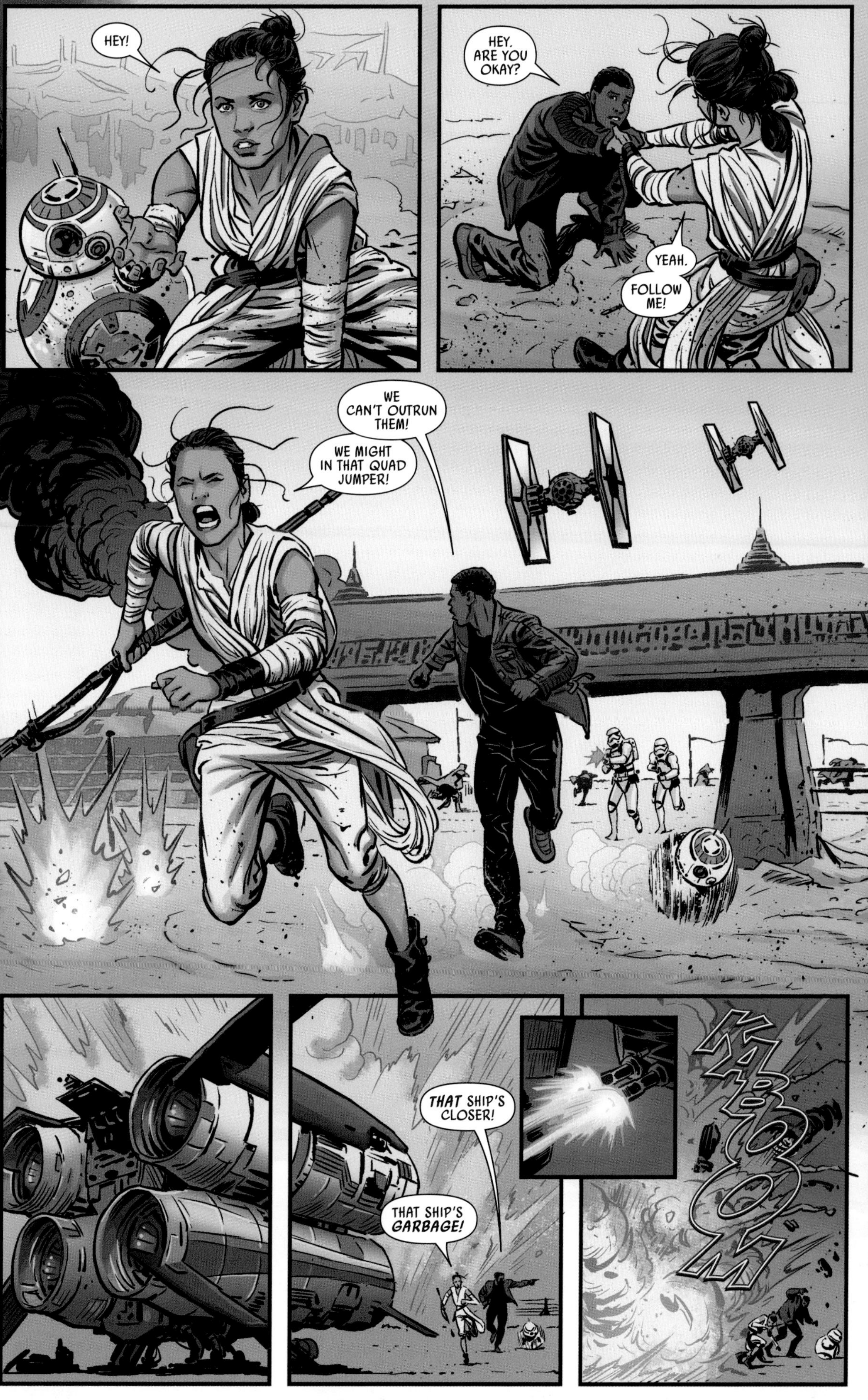
HEY!
HEY. ARE YOU OKAY?
YEAH.
FOLLOW ME!
WE CAN'T OUTRUN THEM!
WE MIGHT IN THAT QUAD JUMPER!
THAT SHIP'S GARBAGE!
THAT SHIP'S CLOSER!
KABOOM

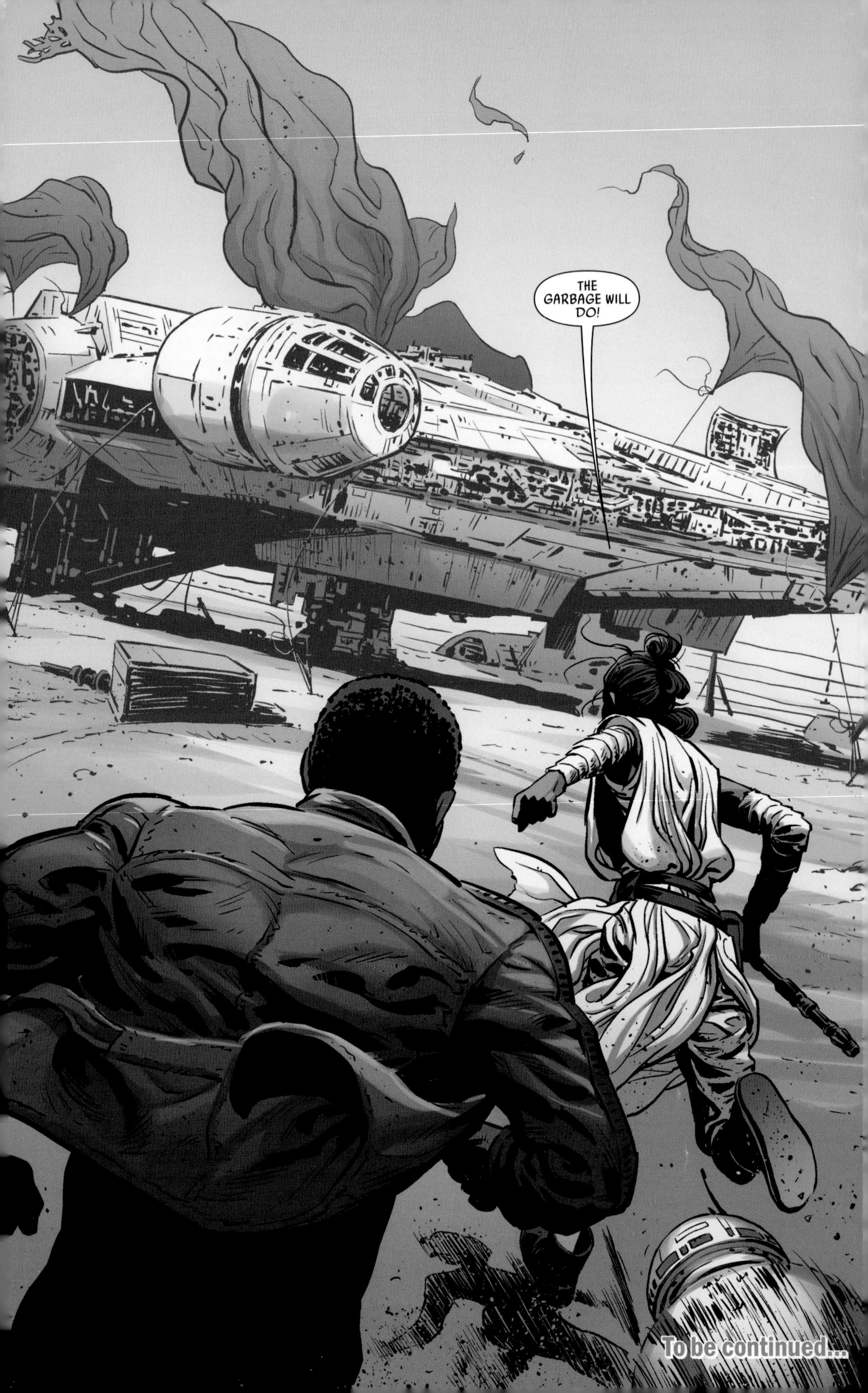
THE GARBAGE WILL DO!
To be continued...